T0158166

EMILY
and the
Lost City of Urgup

An Adventure in Arabia

GERRY HOTCHKISS

iUniverse, Inc.
Bloomington

Emily and the Lost City of Urgup
An Adventure in Arabia

Copyright © 2012 Gerry Hotchkiss

All rights reserved. No part of this book may be used or reproduced by
any means, graphic, electronic, or mechanical, including photocopying,
recording, taping or by any information storage retrieval system
without the written permission of the publisher except in the case
of brief quotations embodied in critical articles and reviews.

This is a work of fiction. All of the characters, names, incidents,
organizations, and dialogue in this novel are either the products
of the author's imagination or are used fictitiously.

iUniverse books may be ordered through booksellers or by contacting:

iUniverse
1663 Liberty Drive
Bloomington, IN 47403
www.iuniverse.com
1-800-Authors (1-800-288-4677)

Because of the dynamic nature of the Internet, any Web addresses or
links contained in this book may have changed since publication and
may no longer be valid. The views expressed in this work are solely those
of the author and do not necessarily reflect the views of the publisher,
and the publisher hereby disclaims any responsibility for them.

Any people depicted in stock imagery provided by Thinkstock are models,
and such images are being used for illustrative purposes only.

Certain stock imagery © Thinkstock.

ISBN: 978-1-4759-3762-6 (sc)
ISBN: 978-1-4759-3764-0 (hc)
ISBN: 978-1-4759-3763-3 (e)

Library of Congress Control Number: 2012912267

Printed in the United States of America

iUniverse rev. date: 9/11/2012

Dedicated to
Abby, Claire, Lilly and Zoe

Introduction

Archaeology is the study of ancient cultures. In South and Central America there were the Mayans, the Oltecs, the Toltecs and the Aztecs. In the United States, there was a great city few have ever heard about. Cahokia, a mound city with outlying villages on the East side of the Mississippi near St. Louis. At one time, more than 20,000 people lived there when London, England had but 10,000 inhabitants. The mighty Mississippi's banks overflowed in the hundreds of years before Western Man arrived and its people dispersed to higher ground leaving most of its story buried or lost.

The early Egyptian civilizations were the prize of archaeology with their Great Pyramids and nearby, The Sphinx. Even today, new sites are being uncovered beneath the sands of time.

This story takes place in the early 1920's when American archaeologists joined in on the hunt in The Middle East to discover civilizations written about in ancient papyrus but never located.

Contents

CHAPTER ONE:

To Be Made A Fool Of

EMILY DARROW LIVED in a small New England town. It had a college where her father was a Professor of English and her mother was the town's librarian. So it was not a surprise that her house was full of books. Books were found in virtually every room of the house, even the bathroom. Where there were no books there were newspapers and magazines.

"Mom," Emily said to her mother, "do you know what my friends call our house? 'Emily's bookends', because we have wall to wall books."

"Well, it's better than being called the house of the do-nothings," her mother replied. School had just ended for the summer and her mother was preparing dinner. "Would you add another chair to the dining room table, Dad's invited some old Professor to dinner." "A roommate of your grandfather's when he was at college," she went on. "By the way, take off those scruffy blue shorts and purple shirt and put on your Liberty Lawn dress with the white collar, it goes so well with your blue eyes and hair. Emily's father called it "dirty brown", which she hated. Her hair wasn't dirty, just a mixture of blonde and brunette colors. Emily had on her dreamy look, as though she were gazing off at some far distance, as she climbed the stairs to her bedroom. Her mother would say, "Emily's in another world." She changed clothes. Her dress came down four inches from the floor and showed off her new white sandals, shoes that were both comfortable and practical. She was the second tallest girl in her classroom and still growing.

"With school out, what shall I do this summer?" Emily mused. New England summers always started out well, but by August the hot sun and the long days never ended. By then, she couldn't wait to get back to school and see all of her friends.

"Well hello, my favorite girl, why the pensive look?" asked her father as he walked into the house. "I was just thinking about what to do this summer," she answered, giving her father a big hug and squeeze until he pretended to be out of breath.

"If your mother agrees, I may have a great surprise in store for you this summer," her father told her, "but it will have to wait until Witherspoon arrives." "Witherspoon?" she asked. "He is a very special man, you might even say a very great man and you will meet him soon," her father relied.

Emily wanted to know the secret her father wouldn't mention but she bit her tongue and helped her mother set the table for five people. Her mother and father, her baby brother, Seth, and the very important person, Mr. Witherspoon.

When he arrived, he certainly didn't look important, If the

truth were known, he looked sort of seedy. He took off an old crumpled hat and his white hair sat on the top of his head going this way and that way. He was skinny so the collar of his shirt sagged away from his neck and he had a small mustache that covered his upper lip and below that not much of a chin at all. His tweed coat hung loosely and his arms hung well beneath the cuffs of the coat. His shoes needed polishing unlike Emily's father who kept them as shiny as when he was a marine in the Great War.

A small pair of glasses covered most of Mr. Witherspoon's eyes, but when he looked straight at Emily, the smile on his face, the twinkle in his eyes, the energy that seemed to explode from his trim frame captured Emily by surprise. She seemed overwhelmed. He seemed full of joy!

"You must be the Emily I have heard so much about from your granddad," he noted. "I am Professor Ernest G. Witherspoon, your most humble servant." What could Emily say after such a strange introduction. She put out her hand which was clasped into what Emily felt was a very strong grip, indeed. So she squeezed back as hard as she could. The professor laughed.

Before dessert, when coffee was being served, Emily's dad got up, went into the den and returned with a sheaf of papers. "Sarah, please come and sit down," he said to her mother. "Professor Witherspoon has something special to propose to us."

"Ernest, please, Ernest," said the professor. Then he went on, "as you know, I am an archaeologist, having spent my lifetime studying ancient civilizations. Early this year I received an invitation from a colleague of mine in Egypt to come to Arabia and look for what we believe to be important lost cities. I plan to be there from the middle of June until August 15th, two months. And I would like to take Emily along with me."

"Emily?" queried her mother. "A twelve year old is to go away, across half the world, with an almost sixty year old man I have never met before, for two whole months." "Is this some sort of joke?" she went on.

Emily's father had heard how abrupt Professor Witherspoon was known to be, but he hadn't expected him to offer quite that simple an explanation. "Sarah," he said, "let me elaborate, if I may." "This idea isn't some sort of last minute concoction. Ernest and my dad and I have talked about it for months. The Middle East is the beginning of our civilization, our culture, our art, and our writing. You know how Emily is always being teased by her friends about the books and magazines and newspapers that clutter this house. Here is a golden opportunity for her to see how it all started. The very roots of our love of literature."

He had reached the core of Emily's mother's heart and soul.

"Put yourself at Emily's age. Wouldn't you have died for such an opportunity?" he added.

He had angled out the perfect fly for Sarah. Now he had to wait and see if she would take it and then be very careful pulling her into his net. "Okay, let's talk about it," she said.

Emily was confused. She had always been told not to go out with any stranger and Professor Witherspoon was certainly a stranger to her. The trip to Arabia sounded so exciting. What could she do?

She remembered the stories of knights from foreign lands who wanted to marry a king's daughter. The knights had to perform all sorts of tests to win her hand. She decided that if the Professor wanted to take her on the trip, he would have to pass four tests. Skipping rope, jacks, hop scotch and, she thought for a minute, a brain test, 'I packed my grandmother's trunk'.

She proposed the tests to Professor Witherspoon. He looked at her with a bemused and quizzical face. "You will discover, Emily, that I am not the most coordinated person you may have the pleasure of knowing. But I shall try my best."

She went to her bedroom and in the closet underneath shoes and books and clothes she hadn't put away properly she found a jumping rope and a set of jacks. They went out side. "The first test," announced Emily, "will be the Jumping Rope Test." "Watch me." She jumped 'one, two' on both feet and then "three, four' on first her right and then her left foot. Professor Witherspoon tried but the rope was too short and it hit the back of his neck.

"Jacks, will be the second test," Emily decided. She rolled the jacks in a tight grouping on the sidewalk by her house. She tossed the small red ball up in the air, picked up one jack and caught the ball. Then she gave it to the professor. He tossed the ball so high it bounced off the limb of a maple tree overhead and landed in the gutter of her house, rolled down a gutter pipe and into the prickly bushes. By the time they found some work gloves in the garage to use to get the ball out of the prickers, Emily decided to move on to test three, Hop Scotch.

She went up stairs to Seth's room where he had a blackboard on a stand. She found a piece of chalk and scampered back down, outside to the sidewalk. She drew a pattern of squares on the sidewalk then looked around for a small flat stone. Explaining the game to the professor, she tossed the stone onto a square and then, on one leg, hopped onto another square and bending over on one leg retrieved the stone. The professor's turn came next. He took the stone in his hand. It disappeared between has long fingers and thumb. Then he flipped it like a marble and it sailed out of sight. This happened with three other stones and Emily gave up the test.

There was only one test left and so far the professor had not passed even one of the others. She explained that she and the professor would "pack my grandmother's trunk' with either fruits or vegetables starting with the letter 'A' and going through the alphabet ending with "Z". Each person had to remember all the fruits and vegetables. She started. "I packed my grandmother's trunk and in it I placed an apple." He went on, "I packed my grandmother's trunk and in it I placed an apple and a banana." When Emily got to the letter I, she seemed stuck. She said timidly, knowing the answer wasn't exactly proper, "Idaho potato. "Well done," said the professor. This surprised Emily; her father would have protested that answer.

His letter 'J' was jicama which was sounded with an 'H', not a 'J' He explained that jicama was a tuberous root of the pea family and when eaten raw in salads in the Southwest tasted quite sweet. They continued on. Emily was astounded how quickly the professor rattled off the fruits and vegetables in a staccato voice without ever pausing to remember one. But he got the letter 'X'. The dreaded letter. Even her father lost when he got 'X'. He paused, as if he were reading the dictionary in his mind. "Aha," he said, "although I am not sure this is really proper." Then he added 'xanthan gum', a natural gum used by companies to stabilize manufactured foods.

Finally he got 'Z', the other tough letter. "Zinfandel," he completed the alphabet proudly, explaining it was a black grape used in making wine. Emily beamed. Not because he finally passed one of her tests. Rather that in each she had learned more and more about this older friend of her grandfather's. He was awkward and he was shy. But he was modest and incredibly bright and most important of all, he was so kind and gentle and thoughtful. He had all the attributes one would wish for in a friend.

Even her mother was taken by the professor. Watching him attempt to pass her daughter's tests without ever being condescending, she saw a wonderful teacher.

The professor outlined the trip. He and Emily would sail on the lie de France from Boston to Le Havre on the 15th of June. The sailing would take six days. From there they would take a train to Marseilles to board a smaller boat of the French Line and sail to Beirut in Lebanon. Professor Dasam would meet them there to arrange the rest of the journey.

To insure that Emily used the time to good advantage, the professor had hired a Madam Babbette Boissiere to instruct her in French, which was the main language of the Levant, although they would for the most part be in Arabia.

Sarah looked at her daughter, her eager eyes, her imploring face. How could she deny Emily a trip of a lifetime.' "All right," she said, "but Ernest, if anything happens to Emily I will go to the farthest corner of the globe, put you in stocks in the middle of the

Boston Commons for everyone to mock you. Do you understand me." Emily had never heard her mother talk like that. Even her father looked totally surprised. "A little over-dramatic, but I think the professor understands your feelings, Sarah," he commented.

"What are stocks?" Emily asked. "It means, dear girl, should I not return you safe and sound, your mother will have me placed with my face and hands and feet sticking out through wooden holes in a fence, to be made a fool of by every person passing by," Witherspoon answered.

Even her mother was embarrassed by his description.

CHAPTER TWO:

"You Naughty Boy"

THE DAYS FLEW by as Emily prepared for her summer in Arabia with Professor Witherspoon. Her father bought her a large steamer trunk and her mother packed her clothes for two months. The days would be hot, so she had shorter skirts and cotton blouses and socks that would go up to her knees. The nights would be cold, so she had warm woolen nightgowns, sweaters, long dresses and full length sleeves on her blouses. She even had a hat with an very large brim that was wider than her shoulders. Her mother said it was to keep the sun off her pale face.

She also packed several quarts of maple syrup as presents to Professor Dasam and Madam Boissiere. Her dad said that they would enjoy them because there were no maple trees in that part of the world. Emily thought about that - how sad not to see the glorious colors of Fall when the maple trees turned every color of yellow and orange and red.

The day before the ship left, Emily and her father and Professor

Witherspoon drove to Boston and stayed at an elegant hotel called the Ritz Carleton. Her mother stayed at home with Seth and when she hugged and kissed Emily goodbye, Emily could feel a shudder and gasp in her mother's voice as she whispered, "I love you, my dearest, and I shall count the days until you come home."

Boston was so much bigger than Emily's town. Around the Commons there were several churches, hotels, stables for horses, garages for automobiles, a pond with swans and a place to rent row boats. Do you know why they call this area the "Commons"? Professor Witherspoon asked and then answered. "Originally this was common land for all the people of Boston to feed their sheep and goats and cows. Later on when the number of citizens of Boston were too many for all of them to use the Commons, they made it a park.

At ten o'clock the following morning, Emily and Professor Witherspoon boarded the great French liner called the Ile de France. They were traveling "Cabin Class" which was the middle of three classes of state rooms on the boat. The top was called "First Class" and it was reserved for the very richest travelers. The bottom was called "Third Class, which was the least expensive and popular with students and poor families returning home.

As Emily entered her stateroom, she smelled an elegant perfume and turned to her left to see before the most beautiful older woman she had ever met. Her silver hair was piled high into an unusual knot, the lashes of her eyes twice the size of Emily's mother's, outlining large brown eyes. She had high rouged cheekbones and bright red lipstick which should have looked garish but didn't on this lady. Her one detraction was her size. She was hardly taller than Emily

"Emilie, ah mon chere," she said. "I am Madam Babbette Boissiere, but you shall call me Madam Bibi." "It is now 10:45 AM and your first French lesson will begin at 11:30 AM so that we can lunch at the last sitting at 2:15 PM like civilized persons." With that Madam Bibi left the state room. "Civilized persons," thought Emily. She had never eaten lunch that late in her life and she did not appreciate Madam Bibi's suggestion that she and her mother and father were uncivilized.

Nevertheless, at 11:30 Am sharp Madam Bibi arrived at the state room and took Emily to another room for her lessons. "This is the card room," Madam Bibi explained, "but it is not used before the afternoon so it will be our classroom." Emily has never studied a foreign language before and had not the faintest idea how the studies would be done. She soon learned. like English there were verbs and nouns and all of the other words that modified them but there was much more which Madam Bibi taught with the most engaging manner. She would always place her French in some context of Emily's life or what she approved of for Emily's life.

After lunch, there was a short nap followed by lessons so that they would also eat dinner at 10:00 PM "like civilized persons". Even Professor Witherspoon accepted the Madam's dictates. As he told Emily aside, "you know the French are famous for their cooking."

Not only was lunch and dinner eaten quite late, but Madam Bibi had strict ideas of what "civilized persons" ate. Much of it Emily loved, but when she discovered that she was eating the brains or the pancreas or even the intestines of an animal, she lost her appetite and asked to be excused one evening.

"Ah, Professor," said Madam Bibi, "you Americans have such limited minds, such peasant tastes, such lack of adventure in food." "I suppose you could call us "meat and potatoes," he answered, "and please call me Ernest." "Ah, we shall change that, mon chere Ernest," she replied. "There is a dance this evening. Would you care to escort me?" she went on.

Professor Witherspoon was flabbergasted. Such brazen behavior to almost force him into dancing. Outrageous. He looked at Bibi, who gave him her best fluttering eyelashes, and said, "I would be delighted."

Having gone to bed without supper, Emily found herself very hungry. She peered out of her state room just as a porter was passing. "May I do something for you, miss?" he asked. Emily explained how she had not dined and was hungry. "We can fix that," he answered. "Put on your shoes and follow me." They went past the dining room into a large ballroom with chandeliers lit with hundreds of lights, chairs in plush red fabrics, tables filled with candles and glasses of wine. Couples were dressed in black tie and evening gowns, either talking at the tables or dancing.

The porter put Emily at a small table in a corner where she could see but not be seen too well. In a few minutes he returned with a plate full of smoked salmon, cheeses, cold cuts, small pickles, butter, bread and a glass of milk. "Bon Appetite," he announced and left. While Emily ate, she suddenly spied Madam Bibi and the professor dancing. He seemed quite awkward, often tripping over Madam Bibi's elegant tiny slippers. She heard the Madam say, "Oh you naughty boy!" when the professor tripped. "How could she address him as if he were a child," Emily thought.

By the time Emily finished her meal she was so tired it took all her effort to find her state room and drop into her bed, fully clothed.

But she awoke with a start the next morning as the ships bells and horns blew. Already dressed she stepped out into the corridor to find both Madam Bibi and the professor dressed and carrying large orange vests with them. "Ah, mon chere," said Madam Bibi, "you are a clever girl to dress so quickly for the fire drill. Put this on and follow us onto the deck." An officer of the ship, with his uniform showing two stripes around his cuffs, explained what to do if the ship should catch fire. They would be put in the life boats that were secured on the sides of the deck.

After the drill, all three went to eat breakfast. "A barbaric rite, Ernest," said Madam Bibi. "I shall have a croissant and coffee in my room, if you will please excuse me," she added as she marched out of the dining room. The professor seemed more amused than surprised and winked at Emily. Emily drank her orange juice and looked forward to her bacon and eggs.

The lessons went well. French was fun. But even more fun was the strange way Madam Bibi spoke English. "Professor Witherspoon is more than meets the eyes, yes?" she noted. "How can somebody be more than meets the eyes?" Emily wondered.

Emily's French had advanced much faster than Bibi had imagined. So much so that before an afternoon lesson when Emily asked about Bibi's life, she decided to tell Emily about life in France.

"My father was an army officer. He was a second son and in Europe the second son does not inherit as does the first, so he often joins the army.

"Inherit?" asked Emily.

"The family estate, in our family it would be my father's vineyard in Bordeaux. So my father went to Saint Cyr, the great military academy, like your West Point. It was difficult for him because his family were Huguenots."

"Huguenots?" Emily asked again.

"Protestants. You know France is a Catholic country, and my mother came from a very strict Catholic family. So there was quite a fuss about the marriage of their daughter brought up in schools run by Nuns marrying not just a religious non-believer but a Protestant as well. But my grandfather was really a non-believer and he adored my father.

I was told he said to my grandmother, "which do you prefer, a boring, unimaginative son-in-law who attends matins every afternoon or a well educated, amusing, alert, questioning young man who adores our daughter and is quite willing to be instructed by Priests even though you know he has no real interest in any religion." I think my father had already won over my grandmother, so they were married."

"As you know, the Great War came when I was thirty-six. An old maid, as you would say.

"You could never have been an old Maid," exclaimed Emily.

"Well, it is an old and sad story. I was once in love, when I was eighteen. He was an officer in my father's company. Not really a soldier, he was a physician. Tall, angly, shy, not unlike the

14

professor, with dark hair and eyes that sparkled. We were in love, but when he proposed to marry me, everything fell apart. Phillipe was Jewish and his parents were absolute that he marry within his religion. Mine were so very different. I don't think they cared much about religion. If you love him and he loves you and he is a good man was all they wished. But to be fair to Phillipe's parents, there was very little intercourse between these religions. How shall I explain it. Christians and Jews lived separately and if not spoken aloud there was a distinct aloofness, a looking down on Jewish people. I am sure they wished to protect him from moving too tightly into such an un-Christain, Christian society. Ah my cher, you look so sad."

"But it is so unfair," said Emily.

"Well, life must go on and I held on to Phillipe for much too long. I did many things but my favorite was studying ballet. I was just a fair student and the men loved me. I was so small and light, they could pick me up and carry me with such little effort.

Now here I was in 1914, when the Great War began. We thought it would be over quickly. Why? I do not know. For me it was. Too soon after that, my father was killed in battle. They were so close, my mother never got over his death and she died less than a year later. My Uncle became my new father and he was, what can I say, the most generous and kindliest stepfather a girl might dream of. With the War raging and, fearing for all of our lives, he pleaded with me to go to America to escape the carnage.

I landed in Ellis Island, where the importer of my uncle's wines, a portly and very attentive man, met me and took me to his home in New York City, a large apartment near Central Park.

What should I do? I thought of so many things but then made a decision. I became a French teacher at a private girl's school, Rosemary Hall, in Greenwich, Connecticut. Con-nec-ti-cut That is a word I still cannot pronounce correctly. What a change for me from remembering my Nuns in their black habits, to joining women teachers in everyday dresses. So, Cher Emily, when I speak correct English, you can thank those ladies, and when I do not, you can blame me, also spending too many weekends in New York City."

"So you became a teacher?"

"Oh no, Cherie, nothing is ever as simple as that. My uncle has made me quite self-sufficient. Enough income to do pretty well what I pleased. It took some time to discover how much I loved teaching. I loved the spirit I found in the young girls. And when this Summer job, as you might call it, teaching you French along with other subjects, came along, I took it as a lark, just for a change. And it is pleasing me more than you shall ever know."

That night Emily lay in bed with tears in her eyes. She could not sleep. What a sad story of Bibi's life. Emily knew that war was terrible. Her father never mentioned it and when she had asked him about it her mother told her never to do that. But what about religion? Was it not about God is love. Why would it separate people's love of each other? And how could Bibi be so full of the love of life now after all it had done to her?

Tomorrow they would land and Emily finally willed herself to sleep.

When they disembarked at Le Havre, the Professor dropped

16

his briefcase. "Oh you naughty boy," said Madam Bibi. And the professor laughed.

The smaller boat to Beirut had none of the elegance of the Ile de France. "It is down and dirty,' commented the Professor. "More dirty, than down," echoed Madam Bibi. But the trip was shorter and when they docked in Beirut, Emily said "adieu" to Madam Bibi who took the professor aside to say their farewells. They would meet again in the beginning of August to return.

CHAPTER THREE:

A Pyramid

WHILE PROFESSOR WITHERSPOON was taking much too long to say good bye to Mada Bibi, Emily looked around the dock to see if she could spot Professor Dasam. There was nobody dressed in Arabic garments to be seen. She was turning around when she heard a high pitched voice call out, "Are you by any chance Miss Emily Darrow?"

Before her stood the opposite of Professor Witherspoon. Where the professor was tall and thin, unkempt and tweedy, the man addressing her was short and fat, impeccably dressed in a dark gray suit, white starched shirt with a striped tie, black shined shoes, a clean shaven face with the bushiest eyebrows Emily had ever seen. "May I introduce myself," he ventured, "I am Professor Demosthenes Dasam."

He led Emily to a large black automobile with a driver in a light gray uniform, white gloves and a matching gray and white cap. The driver opened the rear door and Emily peered in to a sumptuous interior of soft leather and burled wood and enough room for four or five people.

"Aha Dasam, you've met Emily and now I see you are impressing her with your brand new Rolls Royce," said Professor Witherspoon arriving just as Emily entered the limousine. The three sat in the back while the driver placed the luggage from the boat onto a rack on the rear of the automobile. "We're on our way," Dasam exclaimed.

As the car drove south along the Mediterranean Sea, the two professors talked endlessly about archaeology, ancient texts, early civilizations and the possibility of a lost city. Between the rumbling of the car and the incessant chatter of the professors, Emily soon fell fast asleep.

When she awoke, she found her head lying on a pillow on professor Witherspoon's lap. She sat up with a start. "I'm sorry, I must have fallen asleep. What did I miss?" she asked. "About two hours of dusty driving and two hours of boring conversation, my dear," answered Professor Dasam with a twinkle. "But it is lunchtime," he added. Emily looked about. As far as she could see there was nothing but the road, occasional palm and Cyprus trees and the sea at a distance. Where would they dine?

The driver turned down a small dirt road that led towards the sea. In a few minutes they stopped under a grove of palm trees, facing the water. The driver unstrapped the luggage and opened the boot or trunk of the car. He took out a folding table, three chairs, table cloths and napkins, sterling silverware and from a wicker basket an assortment of fruits, nuts, a canister holding cold yogurt and sandwiches.

"Add another chair, Ali," Professor Dasam, requested. "Ali and I have been together for many years and he knows I do not favor the great separation of classes you Westerners prefer."

"Professor Dasam and I were roommates at Cambridge where we both received our PHD's," Professor Witherspoon explained. "He thinks all English speaking people share the same cultural attitudes. He has never been to America and I plan to ask him there to see the vast differences there are between the English-speaking English and the English-speaking Americans."

"In my little town there are English and German and Portuguese and Italian and Irish and two Armenian families who sell Oriental rugs," commented Emily. That seemed to calm the professor and they set to eating a light but tasty meal followed by tea. The driver put everything back into the Rolls Royce and he and his three passengers drove off.

"Let me tell you the bad news, first, Professor," said Dasam. We are certain it exists but we cannot find one thing that might lead us to a lost city." "There are numerous tracts describing the city, but none mention its name or location." "And to add insult to injury, there is a band of thieves also looking for the city, to loot it before we might find it."

By now the limousine had arrived at Dasam's palatial house in Cairo, where Emily and Professor Witherspoon were introduced to Dasam's wife and three children. Not really children at all, since the youngest was nineteen. They were curious about everything American - jazz music, dancing, silent movies, the Edison gramophone. Few things that Emily really knew much about but she embellished a story as best she could. She told them Thomas Edison had invented the electric light bulb and the talking machine that started with round discs but now had large circular records with hundreds of grooves over which a needle moved and turned the grooves into voices and music. But she had no idea how it all really worked.

The Professor's house was filled with rugs and pillows and many servants who were at that time preparing tea. Tired from the long ride in the Rolls Royce, Emily asked to be excused and took a long nap. So long that she didn't wake up until the next morning.

"What shall we do today?" she asked at breakfast. "I thought it would be entertaining and instructive to drive out to see the Great Pyramids of Gaza," said Professor Dasam. Another ride in a car wasn't what Emily had in mind but she was a good sport and agreed enthusiastically.

Halfway to the Pyramids off to the side of the road Professor Witherspoon spotted what looked like a tiny pyramid about three feet tall. "Some child must have dropped his toy, let's pick it up," he suggested. The driver stopped the Rolls Royce and Emily and the professors walked over to pick up the toy. It seemed to be stuck in the sand and after a few tugs the professors agreed to leave it where it lay and let its owner find it.

"Suppose it isn't a toy," said Emily. "Suppose it is the very top of another pyramid covered over with sand, like the tops of icebergs in the North Sea where more than two-thirds are under the water, unseen."

"People have come past here for centuries, Emily, and not seen the top of another pyramid," Professor Dasam remarked.

But Professor Witherspoon was intrigued and he asked the driver of the automobile if he had a shovel. One was produced. "Ernest, you don't really plan to dig out a lost pyramid," said Dasam. "Just a poke here and there," Witherspoon answered.

But the poking turned into something very different. With each shovel-full of sand the "toy" pyramid grew larger and larger until it was more than ten feet across and still growing bigger and bigger. Professor Dasam's eyes also grew bigger and bigger. "Allah be praised, Emily is right. Before us is a new undiscovered pyramid." They all returned to the car and sped back to Cairo, where Professor Dasam called the University and several government officials to close off that section of the desert and organize a proper excavating team.

The news sped all over Egypt and even the rest of the world. In fact just five days later, Emily's mother read about it in her local paper. Its headline read, "Emily Darrow of West Elm Street Has Discovered a Pyramid in Egypt." It went on to note that Emily would enter Seventh Grade in the Fall but said little about the actual discovery. Sarah called the editor but was told he was off for the rest of the day and there was nobody in the news room to help her find out anything more.

At the site of the pyramid were hundreds of men digging and large trucks removing the sand. The work went from dawn to early in the evening while it was still light out. While the men were digging, Professor Dasam showed Emily pictures of the other pyramids and she read about their secret entrances, many rooms, mummies and other objects placed next to the dead kings and queens of ancient Egypt.

While digging at an eastern wall, workers discovered a room or hallway block that suggested a passageway into the pyramid. With careful instructions from Professor Dasam, they unearthed the passage, scraped away all the dirt and found a doorway with two large alabaster cats sitting on either side. The cats were at least twelve feet high with their necks stretched and their faces facing inwards towards the door. "This must be the entrance to the royal tombs," said the professor.

It was. With light from hundreds of candles held by workers, the three entered what turned out to be a square room some ninety feet across each direction. In niches in the walls were statues of men and women all facing towards one larger niche in which a small box lay on a golden stone.

The box was no larger than a candy jar, but it was encrusted with precious stones overlayed with gold. "May I touch it," Emily asked. "Normally, I would say no, but this is your discovery. Put on your gloves and pick it up, if you wish," Professor Dasam replied.

It was quite heavy for its size but easily picked up. The professors decided to take the box back to Cairo. On the return they all took turns trying to open the box, but there seemed to be no key hole, or notch or any opening they could find. Along the top were numerals from 1 to 12. "Surely this is the key to opening the box," thought Emily. "Is twelve an important number, Professor Dasam?" she asked. "Rather important, but nowhere near as important as nine," he answered.

Emily took the box in her hands and counted from left to right to the number nine and pushed. Nothing happened. Then she counted from the right to the left nine times to the number four and she heard a faint "click". She tried the nine again and there was another "click" but nothing happened. So she counted halfway from the right to seven and pushed. Another click. She counted from the left to six and pushed.

The box flew open.

The Professors shot up in their car seats and called to the driver to stop the car. The three of them peered into the box. It was empty save for a small piece of parchment. Professor Dasam attempted to read the hieroglyphics:

"We of the Glorious City of Urgup dedicate this tomb to all its peoples that they may lie here on their journey to the other —," he could not make out the next part of the text. "— leagues from — where the sun sets on — a camel's day from Ur."

"Our lost city has been found, Emily," he said, " or rather it has been named.

"Urgup"

CHAPTER FOUR:

The Colour of Kidnappers

THE NEWSPAPER ARTICLE about the new pyramid lay on a table in a rundown hotel at the outskirts of Cairo. A place frequented by riffraff, thieves, cutthroats, bunko men and drifters. Among them were four noticeably different men. Noticeable because they were English from the East End of London and they kept just to themselves. Their leader, Smily Wiley, had a round face which was centered by a waxed moustache that curled well beyond his cheeks. Butts, a companion in crime, had chopped whiskers that ran down the sides of his face. Rutts, another, seemed to have a perpetual three week's growth of scraggly beard and droopy eyelids. Nutts, the third, was completely bald.

"Look here, Smiley," said Butts. "The American girl has spotted a brand new pyramid." "Let's rob it while it's fresh from the sands," laughed Rutts. "Forget about the pyramid. There will be bobbies all over the place guarding its entrance." "Now, I have a better idea. We'll kidnap the girl and ransom her for the loot inside the pyramid."

"But she's just a little tyke," said Nutts, "why would you go and do a thing like that?"

"Always the soft heart," said Smiley Wiley. "Tell you what I'll do. When we kidnap her, you can keep watch over her to see that nothing bad happens to her," he added with a chuckle.

The four of them bought an old jalopy missing its headlights and a rear bumper. They filled it full of petrol, which is what they call gasoline in Egypt, and drove off into the desert. Asking several people on the way, they eventually arrived at the site of the newly discovered pyramid. Parking the car a quarter of a mile from the site, they ambled over to watch the digging and to find Emily. They spotted her talking to two older men. She left the men and walked towards a series of tents, so the four thieves followed her. The tents were latrines, toilets, marked "Ladies" and "Gentlemen" and "Workers".

Butts wanted to relieve himself, but Smiley Wiley told him to wait. They had more important work to do than his needs.

When Emily left the "Ladies" tent, the four men grabbed her, stuffing a dirty handkerchief in her mouth so she could not yell, and pretended to be talking to her as they started towards their car. Butts and Rutts said they couldn't wait, they had to go to the bathroom. Smiley agreed. They left Emily with Nutts as they sought out the "Gentlemen's" latrine. "Just a moment," a voice called out, "that tent is for 'Gentlemen', you three can use those tents at the far end signed 'Workers'."

Nutts had a rope with which he tied Emily's hands. "You are

making a square knot," Emily told him. "You want a granny knot to secure my hands," she went on. "A granny. Who taught you, your granny?" asked Nutts, who knew very little about knots. So he untied the square knot, which Emily knew would really secure her, and tied a granny under Emily's careful supervision. Then he tied her to a tree, because he, too, needed to relieve himself.

While the four men were in the 'Worker's tents, Emily easily loosened the granny knot and ran off back to the professors. She did not tell them what had happened because she had lied to Nutts about the knots and knew it was wrong to lie.

What she didn't know, was that Smiley Wiley had already written the kidnap letter and mailed it to the professors, presuming that he would have Emily in capture well before the letter arrived.

When, three days later, Professor Witherspoon received the letter and read it, he was alarmed. "Dasam," he announced, "look at this. Somebody claims he has kidnapped Emily. I thought she was at your house." The two professors raced to Professor Dasam's house only to find Emily in the parlor reading a book on ancient Arabia.

"Emily," they cried out, "thank goodness you are safe." "Safe from what," asked Dasam's wife as she entered the room. "Kidnappers, claiming they had Emily and demanding all the valued property from the newly discovered pyramid in exchange for Emily," Dasam explained and showed his wife and Emily the letter.

"They must be English," Emily said. "How can you tell?" asked Professor Witherspoon. "Because they spell color with a u, colour," she explained. Witherspoon looked at Emily. "Why would she presume the kidnappers were English, when they just as easily might have been Egyptians or Europeans?" he thought. But he let it pass.

"I shall place my two most trusted guards to watch over Emily," announced Professor Dasam. He sent for the men he called Hadar and Kadar. Kadar was at least six feet six inches tall with bushy eyebrows like the professor's. But his body was lean and he had a very embracing smile that lit up his face. Hadar was shorter, darker and more muscular with an enormous moustache that covered half his face. Tucked into his waist Emily spied what looked like a curled sword.

"Ah, you are looking at my scimitar," noted Hadar. "I rarely use it, but I always carry it.," he added. May I see it," she asked. But before Hadar removed the sword from its case, Professor Dasam spoke out. "In this country, Emily, when a man unsheathes his scimitar, he must draw blood."

Despite Dasam's comments, Hadar withdrew the sword from its scabbard and placed it gently into Emily's hands. It was a short sword, curled in an arc and she could feel that the blade was razor sharp.

Before placing the scimitar back in its case, Hadar gave a quick wipe of the blade to his forearm and then wiped the blood from his arm with a handkerchief. Emily was speechless.

"Now," said Professor Witherspoon, "that you have seen the courage of Hadar, I would like to see the courage of Emily. Tell us about the kidnappers, please."

"How did he know?" she wondered and then told the whole story of the failed kidnapping.

CHAPTER FIVE:

The Reign of Hotemhotem

Professor Dasam was head of the Department of Archaeology at the University in Cairo and an expert in hieroglyphics. He took Emily's parchment, unfolded it to read the sign language.

"No," he announced. "This is Emily's and before I read it, I shall teach her the ancient languages of Arabia.

Thus Emily became the youngest student in the Professor's classroom. She worked very hard, repeating words and memorizing signs, studying ancient scripts, questioning translations. A miracle presented itself before Professor Dasam's eyes as Emily excelled beyond almost all of his classroom of students twice her age.

The day came when Emily graduated. "Now," said Professor Dasam, as a prize for your good work, you shall translate the parchment." "No, no," exclaimed Emily, "as a present from me to you, for your great scholarship and love of teaching, I wish you to translate." "Very well," he replied.

"How interesting," he announced. "This talks about a city

called Urgup, the home of Hotemhotem and his wife Nefertutti. It numbers the buildings and the people, the warehouses full of wheat and barley, the fields full of flowers and the stalls for one thousand camels. It talks of Ashtar and Isis, and of the promise of peace on earth."

"Look here, Professor Witherspoon, near the bottom of the parchment is a map. It locates the city near the great Holy Well of Shambac." he added. "Emily, what a great find you have. We know the Holy Well and maybe, if we are lucky, we shall discover the Lost City of Urgup," the professor told her.

The two professors organized a small caravan of camels and a dozen servants to carry them to the Holy Well and scout the area for the lost city. On the day of departure, Professor Dasam, his able assistant, Panwar, and the servants went to a nearby Mosque. There they took off their shoes and washed their feet and hands before entering the building which was conical in shape with a large dome. "They will pray that Allah will guide us safely and that his will be done," noted Professor Witherspoon. "We also say, thy will be done," commented Emily. "Well, of course," noted the professor, "we are all part of the religions that began with Abraham, although sometimes it doesn't appear to be the case."

Emily had never ridden a camel and when the driver of the caravan approached her she was nervous. The camel seemed unconcerned. It was dressed with all sorts of finery across its back and around its face with tassels on blankets and harnesses and even the seat at the top of its hump. The driver spoke to the camel and it kneeled down, first with its forelegs and then its back legs. Emily was helped up onto the seat and with a loud "Hup!

Hup!" the camel rose and Emily found herself sitting higher than the first story of a building nearby.

Off they went and it wasn't long before Emily actually enjoyed the camel ride, swaying this way and that with so much to see high above the street level. Soon they were in the desert leaving Cairo behind in the dusk of evening. They arrived at a small town and booked rooms at an inn beside another Mosque. Emily's room was small but clean and she soon fell asleep only to be awakened in the middle of the night by a voice, a singsong voice, calling strange words in Arabic. There seemed to be echoes everywhere, then silence.

In the morning she asked the professors what the voice was that awakened her in the early hours. "You heard a Messim," explained Professor Dasam; "he call us to prayers five times each day, to remind us that Allah, or God as you would call him, is great and we must honor him by trying to live a life worthy of his greatness."

The next afternoon the small caravan arrived at the Holy Well of Shambac. It was an oasis, a large garden filled with palm trees and fragrant bushes, surrounded by many tents. In front of the tents, tables were set up selling fruits and nuts and every sort of tea. The professors' party set up their own tent not too far away, bought tea and boiled fresh water from the well.

When they had their fill, Professor Witherspoon took out Emily's parchment and he and Professor Dasam studied it carefully, looking this way and that way. As they examined the parchment a small gust of wind arose and swiped the parchment right out of Professor Witherspoon's hands, where it swooped this way and that way and suddenly stopped, dropping it down the Holy Well.

"Oh dear, oh dear," exclaimed the professor, "what shall we do?"

Emily looked down the well. All she could see was darkness surrounded by the stones that had been placed on all sides deep into the sands of the desert. Above was a bucket about two and one half feet in diameter and three feet deep. It was attached by rope to a metal frame which was above and on two sides of the well.

The parchment is made of animal skin, thought Emily. "That means it won't sink right away. Maybe I can go down the well and retrieve it." The idea actually frightened her. Were there spiders and snakes and all sorts of creepy crawlies down there? And suppose the bucket overturned and sent her right to the bottom into the water!

Emily steeled herself and approached the two professors. She told them her plan. Neither liked the idea. It was too risky. She was too young. The parchment probably was already under water.

"But suppose it isn't. It's made of some animal skin. Please, please let me try. We can't give up finding the Lost City or Urgup," she pleaded. The professors thought long and hard. "All right," they said, "we'll give it a try."

Emily climbed into the bucket with her knees tight against her body holding on to the rope with both hands. Slowly the professors and Panwar let down the rope into the well. As she descended the light became darker and darker until she could only see a foot from her hand. After about fifty feet Emily noticed that the wall of the well seemed to change in tone and color, as if the well housing was made of a different material.

Then she noticed what looked like writing on the insides of the well. Soon she could hear water below and then she jerked the rope to let the professors and Panwar stop lowering her. Just under the bucket the parchment floated in the water. Emily leaned over to get it. The bucket twisted and Emily found herself out of the bucket holding onto the rope just inches above the water. She crawled up the rope, hand over hand, until the bucket righted itself. Then she carefully lowered herself back into the bucket. This time, very slowly and carefully she reached down and caught the parchment.

Three tugs on the rope told the men to pull Emily and the bucket up to the top of the well. They were relieved and so grateful that she was safe and that the parchment had been returned without any harm to its inscriptions or its map.

"Wait," said Emily, "halfway down, the sides of the well are made of a different form of rock and there are rows of hieroglyphic inscriptions around the sides. If you will give me paper and pencil and a good flashlight, I can go back down and copy them."

How could the professors say no? Here she had already risked her life to retrieve the bucket and wanted to go back down to further the research into this ancient place. Emily was given sheaves of paper which she tucked down her blouse. A large flashlight was tied around her waist with enough extra string so that she could hold it in either hand.

Lowering herself carefully, Emily signaled when she sighted the changing tone of the rocks. She turned on the flashlight.

Before her and on every side has writing. Shapes of animals and birds, slashes of designs were dug into the stone. Carefully she tied the flashlight against her neck so that she could free her hands to copy the inscriptions.

It seemed that hours had flown by to the three men holding the rope. They became worried. They wanted to pull Emily up out of the well. Yet she had not signaled them and they could tell by the weight of the rope that she had not fallen out. "We'll give her fifteen more minutes," said Professor Witherspoon, "and then we'll haul her out, like it or not." The other two agreed.

Ten minutes later they felt three tugs and with a look of quiet joy and relieved apprehension they pulled her, almost too quickly, out of the well. Emily looked so tired, Panwar picked her up and carried her straight to her tent. Professor Dasam took her some tea and sweet cakes made from dates and honey while Professor Witherspoon sat quietly by her side holding one hand and promising himself that he would never let this wonderful young lady endanger herself like that again.

Suddenly he took her in his arms and cried. That this shy private man could lose himself like this overwhelmed Emily and she gave him a hug and kiss on his forehead. It seemed to jar the professor who stepped back and apologized to Emily for his emotional outburst. "Professor, next to my mother and father you are the person I love most," Emily told him. And this just seemed to confound the professor more as his face reddened and his hands shook and he said in a very quiet voice, "Thank you."

"This time," said Professor Dasam, " you shall translate the inscriptions you have copied from the well." "If you will help me, I shall be glad to," Emily replied. The two of them worked for almost a week, often rewriting whole passages, trying out different words and translations, for the text was not like any other the professor had seen. "It doesn't make sense," he said one day. "There must be a key we are missing. One symbol that stands for something very different from what it means in other texts."

Emily thought about this. "We know that this well is not too far away from the lost city. Suppose that the bottom of the well once was where I found the inscriptions. Suppose that the well was built by the citizens of Urgup." She told this to the professor. "You may have found the key. Let's look at symbols that repeat themselves quite often. Let's translate them as "the people of Ugup or the city of Urgup or ..."

"The reign of Hotemhotem," interrupted Emily.

There it was, the key to the translation. The professor started reading out loud, "Let the peoples know of the reign of Hotemhotem. Of his great love of peace. Of his palace and comely wife Nefertutti. Of his son, Hotemhotem II. Of the city of Urgup and its one thousand camels. Of the spices and barley and wheat that gathers in its stores. Praise be to Hotemhotem, living one hundred leagues from this water from the heavens as the sun rises in its zenith. Praise to ..." and the professor stopped.

"Witherspoon, do you realize what Emily has found," he called out.

"An exact description of how to find the Lost City of Urgup," Professor Witherspoon answered.

CHAPTER SIX:

The Missing Stones

EMILY SMILED AS she looked at her two guards, Kadar and Hadar, who Professor Witherspoon hired to protect her from the evil men, Smiley Wiley and his three thugs, Butts, Nutts, and Rutts. She had gone down the Holy Well to rescue the parchment that had blown down into the water at the very bottom. And in so doing she had discovered the hieroglyphics halfway down that located the most important building in Urgup.

Now, with the one million dollars that Professor Witherspoon had raised from very rich men and women in America, they were digging and removing the sands of thousands of years, discovering a golden dome shaped building.

Emily was able to open its secret door using the same discovery she had made with the magic box. There were three rows of numbers of twelve each, as follows:

1 2 3 4 5 6 7 8 9 10 11 12
1 2 3 4 5 6 7 8 9 10 11 12
1 2 3 4 5 6 7 8 9 10 11 12

Emily knew that 9 was a magic number in Arabia and she had counted from the right side to the ninth number on the top, which was the number 4. Then she counted from the left side to the number 9 and then on the bottom row she took the middle numbers, first the 7 and then the 6.

When the door was opened, Professor Witherspoon, Professor Dasam and Emily were looking at two large and one small sarcophagi. On each was inscribed glyphs and beautiful pictures of Ibises and cats, with gold and turquoise and rubies and emeralds and lapis lazuli outlining the Pharaoh and his wife and what appeared to be a small child. The gems alone were worth millions of dollars, but as Professor Dasam said, "these tombs are priceless. They are the resting place of Pharaoh Hotemhotem, his wife, Nefertutti and I suspect the young Pharaoh, Hotemhotem II."

Surrounding the caskets were bronze and gold and silver pitchers and urns, giant cats and dozens of statues of men and women, who were the servants and scribes and guards of the royal family.

"What happened to them?" asked Emily.

"We do not know for sure," answered Professor Witherspoon, "but we have a pretty good idea." "In about 2599 BC, there was a great earthquake that rocked the Middle East, causing cities to be destroyed as buildings collapsed and thousands of people died - men, women and children."

"Hotemhotem was a great Pharaoh who believed in peace. He allowed no one to carry arms in the city; no knives or clubs. When his city was rocked by the earthquake, evil people who were jealous or mean, attacked the Pharaoh and his wife and child while they were sleeping and their guards were away helping families, whose houses were destroyed, with food and water," added Professor Dasam.

"Later, the evil people were captured and punished. And the people of Urgup rebuilt their city and placed this great mausoleum in it to commemorate the life of their beloved Pharaoh."

'How did it disappear? asked Emily.

"Over time, over many, many hundreds of years, the land could not support the population. That is, it could not grow enough corn or wheat, it did not have enough water and the people slowly left for other places until none remained and the sands of the desert covered it up until today," Professor Witherspoon explained.

Meanwhile Smiley Wiley and his henchmen had dressed themselves up as Arab workers and when they saw the riches of the sarcophagi, the gold and silver and turquoise and emeralds and rubies and lapis lazuli, their eyes bulged and their mouths watered with greed.

"What'll we do now, boss?' asked Butts. "What do ya think, Buttshead," said Nutts. "We'll steal the tombs," said Rutts. "You three couldn't lift even one of them," commented Smiley Wiley. "We just want the jewels, but we've got to be clever." "How?" asked the three henchmen.

"First we must make fake jewels to replace the real ones, so nobody will notice. Then in the dark of night we'll sneak in and replace the real jewels with the fake ones." "How'll we do that?" chimed in the three men.

"I'll bet the wife of one of Dasam's assistants has clothes with lots of fake stones. So we'll cut off a few from a dress, near the bottom where they won't be noticed," said Smiley Wiley.

The wife of an assistant who worked for the two Professors was the cook and a favorite of Emily's. She was always smiling and would tell Emily stories about Berber Tribes and caravans and holidays when they celebrated the Feast of Abraham in which thousands of young rams were cooked. She told Emily about her wedding to Panwar, who was Professor Dasam's right hand man. How they feasted for nine days and nine nights and danced and sang and played flutes and pipes and drums. How her father had given Panwar seventy-seven camels as her dowry and they now owned seven hundred and seventy seven camels.

One day, Panwar's wife, whose name was Apera, said to Emily, "let me show you my wedding gown and maybe, if I lose a few pounds, I might wear it again." They went to Apera's tent and in a box under several layers of beautiful rugs Apera took out a gossamer gown with layers of silk, embroidered with semiprecious stones that looked like the real ones.

"Oh dear, oh dear," sighed Apera, "look how many of my stones have been lost." "I must be more careful."

"Do you wear this gown very often?" asked Emily. "Oh no," replied Apera, "not since my wedding five years ago."

Emily thought to herself, "then why should those stones be missing", and she kneeled down to inspect the hem of the gown where more of the missing stones had been sewn. "That's funny," thought Emily, "there is no sign of wear or tear, in fact it looks like they were clipped off." But she didn't say anything to Apera lest it disturb the lovely cook.

Just before dark, before the moon rose in the sky, Smiley Wiley and his henchmen, dressed as Arab workers, tarried behind the other workers at the end of the day. They hid in the great mausoleum after everyone had left. They had hidden candles in the pockets of their dress. After the secret door was shut they lit the candles and hurried to the room of the tombs. There they set about removing the jewels from each sarcophagus, replacing them with the semiprecious gems they has cut from Apera's wedding gown. Then they hid out in a corner until the next day when the door was opened and they joined the other workers coming in.

"We shall have to hire guards when we have finished excavating this great building," noted Professor Dasam, "to protect these magnificent tombs from grave robbers." "But how could they ever carry these heavy sarcophagi away without anybody seeing them?" asked Emily.

"Oh the robbers wouldn't steal the whole sarcophagi. Why the jewels alone are worth a fortune," he explained. "They are beautiful just as we see them now," said Emily and she stepped up on a box next to the child's tomb to inspect the jewels more closely. She put on white gloves, which archaeologists use when working with priceless old objects, to touch a ruby the size of her thumb. It rolled right off the tomb on to the floor. Emily was mortified.

"Emily!" Professor Witherspoon commanded, "you must be

extremely careful touching these tombs. Now get right down at once!" "I am very sorry," replied Emily, "really, I hardly touched the ruby." Then she got down on her hands and knees to find the ruby. It was right under Professor Witherspoon's left shoe and she gave it to him.

"Goodness gracious!" he exclaimed, "this isn't a ruby, it's just a semiprecious copy!" Then he and Professor Dasam examined the three tombs finding all of the jewels to be fake. "There must have been grave robbers here centuries ago, I'm afraid," noted Professor Dasam. "How sad, how sad," echoed Professor Witherspoon.

"But why would they bother to replace the stones with fake ones," asked Emily. "Why indeed," noted the Professors, "why indeed." "Whoever took the jewels may be still be here among us. But where did he or she get the fake ones?" they added.

"I think I know," announced Emily and she told them about the missing semiprecious gems from Apera's wedding dress.

CHAPTER SEVEN:

Double Trouble

"Whoever stole the jewels doesn't know that we know they were stolen," Professor Witherspoon noted. "If we keep this quiet among the three of us, the thieves will have no reason to rush to get away."

"Then how shall we find them?" asked Emily.

"Well, since there is little reason for them to try and kidnap Emily, now that they have the jewels, maybe we can employ Hadar and Kadar to help us," said Professor Dasam. "That is, of course, assuming that there is only one set of thieves here in the city, " he added.

"Why don't we dress up Hadar and Kadar as beggars. We can station them by the entrance to the city, so that they can observe anyone leaving," suggested Emily. "A capital idea," added Professor Witherspoon.

Hadar and Kadar, with some reluctance, put on old torn and dirty clothes, sandals ripped with only partial soles remaining.

They looked like such poor bedraggled souls that even Emily had to laugh at their appearance. Their reluctance, however, had little to do with their costume; they were worried more about leaving Emily unguarded. With assurances from the professors, they took up two spots by the fence on either side of the entrance to the city, squatting on their haunches and calling loudly, "Alms for the love of Allah, alms for the love of Allah."

Meanwhile, Smiley Wiley and his three henchmen were gloating over the theft of the jewels. "What'll we do now, boss?" asked Rutts. "We've got all the time in the world, Rutts," replied Smiley. "Nobody knows the jewels have been stolen. So we'll lay low until the right time comes along and then we'll dress ourselves up as wives of some of the workers and slip out the front gate," he added.

"But won't four wives leaving at the same time be too many?" asked Butts. "You're right," Smiley noted. "Maybe just one of us should take the jewels and fence them in Cairo," he added. "Fence them?" questioned Nutts. "What's fence them mean, like we already got a fence surrounding the city." "A fence is a dishonest jeweler, who will buy our gems for half their real value and then sell each piece separately to other jewelers, who won't suspect they were stolen property."

"Who'll go?" asked Rutts. "Any of you know a fence?" queried Smiley. "Not me," "I don't," "Me neither," the three replied. "Then I guess I'll have to do the job," Smiley concurred. "I'll leave now and sell the jewels. You three wait here and leave in a week. We'll meet at the Old Oasis Inn, on the outskirts of Cairo, where we stayed before. Then we'll split the money."

There was so much digging and sifting and noting every shard of pottery, pieces of statues, liths from arrowheads and knives, parts of inscriptions, that Emily and the professors soon put the stolen jewels out of their minds. A box was found containing a parchment listing all the important people who had lived during the reign of Hotemhotem which Emily translated with the help of Professor Dasam. "You have become a first rate translator," the professor announced proudly.

Smiley Wiley snuck in among the worker's tents and stole an old dress. He shaved off his moustache and covered his face with a scarf. Carrying three large leather bags, made from the skins of camels and containing the jewels, he ambled slowly towards the gate.

"Alms for the love of Allah," cried out Kadar as Smiley approached. He gave the beggar a sneer and proceeded through the gate unobserved. There he joined a small caravan of fifteen people and twelve camels, paying its leader to escort him to Cairo.

Days later, a small gang of bandits surprised the caravan, took all the money the passengers held and stole the camels. Smiley was left with his three bags which the bandits did not bother to inspect, as they peered at such an ugly old woman who looked like she needed a shave.

He and the others in the caravan found themselves alone in the sands of the desert without camels and miles from both Cairo and the Lost City of Urgup. The only thing they could see, besides the desert sands and the blue sky, was a single date palm tree, half hidden in the sand a quarter of a mile away. Night came and while the others slept in their clothes, covering themselves as best they could from the chilly night air, Smiley crept away. He scurried towards the date tree and dug a large hole next to it, burying the three bags of jewels. He looked around to be sure nobody saw him and, silently, returned to the others.

Morning came. And with it the hot sun. Thirsty and hungry, the frightened travelers picked up whatever possessions they still held and slowly shuffled westward, away from the horizon, towards Cairo. None noticed Smiley's three missing bags.

CHAPTER EIGHT:

No Honor Among Thieves

IT WAS SIX days before the passengers from the robbed caravan were discovered by another passing caravan. The fifteen men and women had run out of food and water and were delirious, stumbling aimlessly through the desert sands. They were fed and given water and taken to a hospital in Cairo where the men and women were separated into different rooms. When it was discovered that Smiley Wiley, dressed as a woman, was actually a man, the police were called. In questioning Smiley, all he answered in a stuttering manner was "the dddattted jjjewwwles."

So the police had him transferred to a hospital for the insane.

When a week had passed from the day Smiley left the Lost City, Butts, Nutts and Rutts left the other workers early in the morning and walked almost in a run to the city gates, where Kadar and Hadar had just settled in their spots as beggars, "Alms for the love of Allah" they called out as the three henchmen almost tripped over them in their rush to get out. Hadar and Kadar were suspicious and followed the three out into the desert.

The three, although dressed as poor workers, bought three costly camels. Hadar and Kadar were now fairly sure that they were the robbers. They bought two camels and followed the thieves at a distance into Cairo to the Old Oasis Inn, which was a seedy hotel at the eastern edge of the great city. Dressed as beggars, they would never be allowed in even that shabby a place, so they found a clothing store and bought garments more suitable to traveling men. When Hadar and Kadar entered the Old Oasis Inn they overheard the three henchmen ranting and raving.

"Are you sure nobody named Smiley Wiley has been here?" Butts was demanding of the innkeeper. "About six feet tall, no beard," added Rutts. "Carrying three bags made of camel leather," said Nutts.

"Nobody new has been here for weeks," answered the innkeeper, quite afraid of the three threatening men.

"The rat," said Butts, "he's tricked us; he's taken the jewels for himself." "Well we'll track him down, the dirty scum,' said Nutts. "How?' asked Rutts. "We'll question every jeweler in Cairo until we find him," Rutts replied.

Having heard the three thieves, Hadar and Kadar slipped out a side door of the Inn. "One of us will follow them today, so they won't be suspicious," suggested Kadar, "the other the next day, taking turns, until we find the jewels."

Over the next week, neither the three thieves nor the two guards found a jeweler who had seen Smiley Wiley. Hadar decided it was time to go to the police and report what had happened. The police had the thieves arrested for suspicion of robbery but told Hadar they would not be able to hold them for more than three days without proof of their complicity in the crime.

"Has anything unusual happened in the last week?" Kadar inquired of the police. "Let us think," they answered. "Oh yes," one of the policemen replied. "About a week ago fifteen poor men and women who had been robbed were brought in from the desert. They were in a terrible shape and one of them appeared to be truly crazy. He was dressed as a woman and repeatedly mumbled something that sounded like "the dated jewels, the dated jewels." We placed him in an asylum for the insane."

Kadar and Hadar got the address of the asylum and hurried there. The hospital was a recently renovated large building with a lovely lawn surrounded by a high wall protecting it from the street. There were paths around the lawn with benches and palm trees and several nurses dressed in white attending men and women who wore simple smocks and sandals. Hadar inquired about the man who had been brought in dressed as a woman.

"Oh, the poor thing," said an attendant, "he's right over there under the palm tree staring off into the distance. Hadar and Kadar approached Smiley Wiley and one asked Smiley how he felt today. "The dddattted jjjewwels, the dddattted jjjewwels," was all the reply their received.

They returned to the attendant and asked if there was anything in Smiley's possessions when he arrived. "Nothing but an empty water bag," she answered.

"Well, we have the thieves," noted Kadar, "but we haven't got the jewels." "Kadar," said Hadar, the three men in jail will be let out soon and we must report back to the Professors. You stay here and watch the men while I return to the Lost City to get more help."

In the morning, Kadar hired a guide to help him report to him when the three thieves would be let out of jail and Hadar hurried back to the Lost City.

Meanwhile, Professor Witherspoon was in an anxious frame of mind. "Whatever has happened to Emily's guards?" he pondered. He was afraid some terrible harm might have befallen them. "Witherspoon," said Professor Dasam, "do not trouble yourself. I have known those two men for over twenty years and they're more than a match for whatever thieves are involved in this trickery." But he. too, was worried.

There was nothing they could do, so they continued in their excavating of the Lost City of Urgup. But they were more than relieved when at last Hadar arrived back at the Lost City to tell them of the discovery of the four robbers. Over tea in the late afternoon, Hadar described in detail what he and Kadar found in Cairo. Professor Witherspoon and Professor Dasam and Emily pondered the words of Smiley Wiley.

"The dated jewels, the dated jewels."

"Do you think it refers to their antiquity?" asked Professor Witherspoon.

"Did the robbers of the caravan take them?" asked Professor Dasam.

"Had the robbers taken the jewels, why weren't they sold in Cairo," noted Emily. There must be some other answer, she thought.

CHAPTER NINE:

A Lesson in History

Professor Witherspoon and Professor Dasam huddled together away from Emily. "We must locate the stolen gems," said Witherspoon, "but I do not want Emily to be near those dangerous thieves." "Then I shall go to Cairo. Hadar and Kadar and I will follow the thieves until they lead us to the jewels while you and Emily continue the excavation of the Lost City," suggested Professor Dasam.

"That's a good idea, but please be careful, my great friend," Witherspoon replied. Dasam and Hadar left that afternoon for the journey to Cairo. Professor Witherspoon and Emily returned to the workers who were digging into a new site of a very large building.

"Emily," said the Professor, "it is time for you to learn more about the history of these great cities. For the people who lived here gave us so much knowledge of what we now take for granted.

The numbers we use when we add and subtract came from them. But even more important, they gave us writing."

"Not too far from here is a city called Ebla. In its palace was found a room containing clay tablets. On the tablets were recorded 140 years of the history of the city. The main archive room contained about 1,900 tablets. They were kept on wooden shelves. Another room nearby held the tools the scribes used to make the tablets including a bone pen to write on the clay, a stone to erase mistakes and even brick benches to sit on while they were writing."

"In another city was found a parchment of the Vizier Ptah-hotep recording the advice of another Vizier on how to live a good life. Maybe, if we are lucky, we shall find something similar in one of the buildings we are excavating."

"Why did they use clay?" Emily asked.

"Before they discovered how to make parchment which is made from the dried and treated skins of goats and sheep and other animals, they used clay. It was easy to cut letters or symbols into the soft clay before it hardened. And then, of course, the hard clay kept everything intact. In fact, we are very fortunate that they used so much clay. Over the thousands of years since the tablets were written, these cities experienced fires and earthquakes and other disasters that occur even today. The clay tablets just hardened whereas most of the parchments have disappeared, eroded into dust over time."

"Did everybody write?" asked Emily. "Oh no," the Professor replied. "The scribes were among the very few who could write. Even the Pharaohs and other nobles were illiterate. In those times there were farmers and priests, herdsmen and stable masters, soldiers and mercenaries and scribes to serve the ladies and noblemen of the great cities. The scribes were held in high regard."

"At a much later date, in a great city not too far from Cairo was stored one of the rarest treasures ever collected. The Library of Alexandria. It contained the greatest collection of books on all that the Western world knew. Sadly, years later when the Romans sacked that city, the library was burned and with it much of the knowledge of mankind."

"The Western world?" inquired Emily.

"Well, yes, the Western world. There is also a history, much of it even earlier than what we are excavating, in Asia. Two great civilizations separated by the highest mountains in the world grew in their own ways. 1 Over time people traveled across the mountains and traded their wares for the others goods. Today we call those routes the Silk Road because the silk which made such fine and elegant cloth, came from the Far East and was highly prized in the West."

Emily and the professor went back to the new building just being unearthed. The size of the stone pillars holding the extremities of the building's walls suggested that it might be the palace, itself. And as the workers uncovered one of the walls, Emily could make out, faintly, the drawings of figures: of rams and men and women and chariots. "Maybe there will be rooms with clay tablets here," thought Emily, "I hope so."

That night in the tent over a brazier, a bronze pot holding wood and camel dung which served as the fuel for a fire, Emily mused about the strange comments made by the thief who was in the asylum. "The dated jewels." "What could that mean?, she pondered. Emily decided to write down all the facts she knew. First, there were or appeared to be four thieves. One left the Lost City about a week before the others, dressed as a woman. Question. Why. The man joined a caravan which was set upon by bandits who robbed them of their money and the camels. Question. Did the bandits discover the jewels and if they did why didn't they sell them in Cairo? The first thief was sent to an asylum but he did not have any jewels.

Three men left a week later apparently to meet the first thief at an inn in Cairo. The men were very upset when the thief was not at the inn and they talked, rather too loudly, about the jewels. Then they sought stolen gems at every jewelry store in Cairo. But none were found.

Surmise, the first man had the jewels but lost them somewhere between the Lost City and Cairo.

How far had the first thief traveled when the caravan was set to by robbers? Emily asked herself. The police noted the fifteen travelers had been wandering in the dessert for about four days. Emily thought some more. Let's presume that these people were so confused that they traveled about the normal distance of one day in those four days since they did not have camels and they were lost. How long would the trip take normally? she wondered. Emily sought out the Professor who told her the trip usually took about a week.

That means, thought Emily, the robbers were only one day out of Cairo when they stopped that caravan. "Professor Witherspoon," Emily asked, "I would like to go to the Museum in Cairo to see so much of what has been found in other lost cities." "A good idea," the professor replied, "it is time to broaden your knowledge and besides we both need a break from living in these tents. But you must promise me you will not go far from my side. Remember three of those thieves by now have been released from the jail and are free to roam the city."

"I promise," said Emily with her fingers crossed behind her back.

CHAPTER TEN:

A Little White Lie

"EMILY," PROFESSOR WITHERSPOON announced, "I have great news. We shall not have to ride to Cairo on those bumpy camels. A large roadster is available for all of us to ride in. What a relief!"

But Emily wasn't relieved. The camel caravan took a week to get to Cairo, but what about the roadster? How fast would it go. How would she know when they were about one day's camel ride from Cairo.

"How long will it take us?" she asked the professor. "Actually I haven't the faintest notion. Maybe a day or two shorter or a day or two longer than a week," he answered.

Emily was in a pickle. Should she tell the professor the real reason she wanted to go to Cairo - to find the missing jewels*. He might be angry that she was not forthright with him in the first place. Or he might think it a childish whim. Or worse, he might leave her here at the Lost City and go by himself, as a punishment for her not quite telling the truth. Emily decided the best course of action was to say nothing. "Nothing ventured, nothing gained," she once heard her father say.

The tents were taken down, folded and put away in large boxes along with the braziers, cots, bedding and rugs. Food was prepared for the journey together with large leather bags of water and several umbrellas to protect them from the constant sun so fierce in the daytime. Extra blankets were folded for the nights, so cold and ominous with just the sands of the desert and the wind whining under a moonless sky. Tonight was the dark of the moon when everything seemed most dangerous.

Earlier that morning when Emily awoke, she looked outside her tent. There stood the roadster with its large wheels of solid rubber unlike today's tires. There was no air inside to deflate from a puncture. In the front of the engine was an odd looking bar turned at right angles and stuck into the center of the grill. Despite her concerns, Emily was impressed. She inspected the car, the windows that were already open, the doors and running board and radiator cap on top of the hood. She asked the professor what the strange bar was doing, sticking out from the front of the automobile.

"That is a crank, Emily," he answered. "You turn it clockwise until your hear a spurt and a putter. You've turned the motor on. Now I have to be very careful, because I am left-handed and quite often when the engine starts that crank comes flying off right at me. Right-handed people are standing to the left of the crank so if it does fly off, it just flies by them, whereas I am standing on the right side. Right in its path."

I am right handed, Professor," said Emily. "Can I crank the

engine?" "Well, it's not that easy, I am afraid," he answered, "but thank you for the offer."

The professor stood as closely as he could to the middle of the front of the roadster while he cranked. Nothing happened. "Maybe we'll need camels after all," thought Emily. "The engines cold from arriving here last night. I may have to give her several cranks to get her started," the professor commented to nobody in particular. He often was found talking to himself. On the fourth crank the engine caught and rumbled steadily in a noise quite out of place in the desert.

With all the trunks and bags and boxes piled on top, Emily and several servants including her favorite, Apera, the cook, sat in seats behind those of the driver. It was clear to see that Apera was not at all comfortable in the roadster. The noise it made frightened her but she said nothing. The professor announced that he would drive and the driver would sit next to him as navigator, looking at a map they had brought.

"This should take about a week," the navigator told the professor. What a relief came over Emily's eyes until the navigator went on, "unless we hit a sandstorm. They can wreck havoc with an automobile's engine. I have brought along a large tarpaulin to cover the car should that happen."

The professor put on eyeglasses surrounded by leather with an elastic band that went around his head. Then he put his well worn fedora hat with a black band around its brim back on his head. Emily wanted to laugh at the sight but thought better of it.

When the sand under the roadster was hard, the ride was quite comfortable. But when the sand turned soft, the roadster seemed to buck and twist this way and that like a bronco in a rodeo. Emily loved it when it twisted and bumped making her rise off her seat. She felt she was on a roller coaster. But poor Apera hunkered down and picked up her prayer beads, privately praying that Allah would deliver her from this mad contraption.

At night tents were put up, braziers fired, and bedding put on top of rugs over the sand. There were no cots because they would have taken too much room in the automobile. Apera, thanking Allah for bringing her safely this far, cooked dinner for everybody. Lamb stew with date nuts, couscous and a special tea made from ginger roots. Fine dirt from the sand kicked up by the roadster's tires seemed to be everywhere. Of course there was no place to bathe, so each person dusted off another before retiring to bed.

The next day was very much the same as the last day, as the car bumped and twisted over the sands of the desert towards Cairo. Professor Witherspoon and the driver took turns driving and if the truth were told the passengers greatly preferred the driver. At times the professor seemed to let his mind wander and with it the roadster.

It looked like the company would escape any problems until the sixth day when an horrendous sandstorm could be seen gathering dust to the West and coming straight for the travelers' automobile. In the distance, off the track the car was following, the driver spotted a palm tree. He headed there to park the car under the tree to escape the worst of the storm. And he faced the back of the roadster directly into wind from the storm, much as a sailor points his boat into the wind.

All the windows and doors of the roadster were closed as

tightly as possible and the large tarpaulin was wrapped over the whole roadster. Then the driver and Professor Witherspoon got in back with the other passengers, making each seat bench quite crowded.

Winds blew, more ferocious than Emily could ever imagine, rocking the automobile this way and that. At one moment it felt as if the whole car would tip over only to be righted and tipped in the other direction. The tarpaulin was blown away like a kite at the seashore. Despite closing the windows, fine sand crept through, covering everybody. It wasn't until the early hours of the night that the storm passed by and a calm arose that was as eerie as the roaring of the wind had been before. Nobody moved. Listening. Awaiting another storm.

But there was no other storm. In the dark, the passengers alit from the roadster, dusted off their clothes and breathed the cold fresh air outside.

"It is too early to drive on and too late to set up camp," said Professor Witherspoon, "so everybody just make the best of it until morning and daylight."

"I think that palm tree saved us, praise Allah," Apera remarked to Emily. "Isn't it strange that out here away from the birds or insects that might plant a palm seed in the ground that this lonely date palm should be standing," she added. "Date Palm?" asked Emily. "Oh yes," replied Apera. "In another month you will see the dates closely gathered in the branches."

"The dated jewels," Emily mused. "If this tree is about one day's camel march from Cairo, it must have been seen, near where the robbers attacked the caravan. Suppose the thief hid them here by the date tree. "Apera," Emily asked, "would you help me?" "Of course, my dear, "Apera replied, "what can I do?"

Emily explained her suspicion that the jewels were buried near the date tree. "But the sands have added another two feet to the dessert," Apera noted. Nevertheless, the two women sifted sand from the tree to six feet away in every direction. Nothing was found. "Oh dear," sighed Emily, "here I have made you work so hard for nothing. Please forgive me."

"Not at all," said Apera, "there was nothing else to do until daylight anyway and I hate to be idle." "Just think, by tomorrow we shall be in Cairo and I shall be with my beloved Panwar, who has been helping Professor Dasam there."

The roadster seemed to be in good shape. When Professor Witherspoon cranked it a couple of times it caught on and made that rumbling sound all of the passengers had gotten used to, except for Apera who still fingered her prayer beads and implored Allah to see her safely through the ordeal.

"I'm afraid the automobile is stuck quite deeply in the sand," said the driver. "Will everybody get behind the boot and push together." "The boot?" asked Emily. "That is what the English call the trunk of the car and, of course, the English were here well before we Americans," explained the professor.

"One." "Two." "Three, now push," the driver called. At first nothing stirred. The car seemed stuck for life. But suddenly it began to move. "Don't let up," called the driver. And miraculously the roadster rose and rose out of the deep sand until it was about to be level with the desert when suddenly the front tires stopped dead and sank back two feet.

The driver and Professor Witherspoon were befuddled. "Emily," called the professor, "would you crawl under the bonnet, I mean the front hood, and see what might be in the way of the tires."

Emily crawled on her belly under the roadster's radiator between the tires. She scraped sand this way and that way and was about to crawl back out when she felt something. She dug her fingers into the sand. Something was there that felt smooth and it wasn't sand. She dug some more but it was too deep to remove. She crawled out and told the professor there was something there but she could not remove it alone.

The driver asked the passengers to push the front of the roadster back into the sand right on top of the roots of the palm tree When the automobile was backed right against the tree, the driver and Professor Witherspoon and Emily got on their hands knees and looked for the spot Emily had felt before. "Right here," she said.

In no time time at all three large bags made from the skin of a camel were uncovered. The professor opened one bag. "By Jove," he exclaimed, "we have found the stolen jewels." "Let us thank the storm," he added. "And let us thank Allah," added the driver.

"And," said Apera, "let us thank Emily who had an idea that this is where the jewels might be hidden." Apera told them about Emily's idea and how the two of them had looked all over for the jewels, but, of course, couldn't dig near the date palm tree where the roadster was stuck in a pile of sand.

"Emily," asked the professor, "is that why you wanted to go to Cairo?" Emily's eyes looked down at the sand and she seemed unable to speak out. "Yes," she said at last in the quietest voice imaginable.

"Well hurrah for that!" cried out all of the passengers together. Even Professor Witherspoon smiled and a tear came to his eyes as he hugged Emily. "I guess we'll just call that a little white lie," he added.

CHAPTER ELEVEN:

Emily's Falcons

Now that she had found the jewels, Emily thought she would return to the Lost City. But she was in for a different journey. "We are so close to Cairo," said Professor Witherspoon, "let us continue on to visit its great Museum." The professors and Emily secured the jewels with the driver and rode to Professor Dasam's grand house. His children had left, but Emily found Apera there, explaining how to cook exotic dishes to the household staff.

Professor Dasam's wife was pleased to see Emily and showed her several dresses she had directed a seamstress to make for Emily. Dresses are more practical for the hot and arid climate of Cairo. "Dresses," exclaimed Emily, "why they are gowns, beautiful clothes nobody in my town would ever believe existed!" Using rare silks and the finest Egyptian cotton, embroidered with pearls and semi-precious stones, the dresses shimmered in the quiet light that shone inside the house. Emily tried on four separate dresses. They fit her perfectly. They hung down her lithe body several inches from her feet and as she twirled around the light cotton and silks flowed out and then rested back against her legs.

"When may I wear them?" Emily asked. "Any time at all," answered the professor's wife. "Anytime, even to go to the Museum?" Emily went on. "Why, of course, I would not want a guest of mine walking around Cairo looking like a street urchin." If truth be told, the Professor's wife had three sons and no daughters. She was more than delighted to have the opportunity to play mother and dress Emily.

The following day, Professor Dasam escorted Emily to the pride of Cairo, its great Museum, the finest collection of Egyptian history in the world. As Emily approached she saw a huge building with three arched windows on either side of an imposing entrance. Shadowed by palm trees was an extended doorway with an entrance several stories high. Inside she bought a guide book and began reading. "Emily," said Professor Dasam, " you would take years to see and understand what is in this Museum. We have just one week and I shall be your guide book.-

Emily learned that Egypt had once been two separate countries, Upper Egypt and Lower Egypt,. It was unified some 5,000 years ago. She saw the slate palette of King Narmer, the oldest in history. Rooms were filled with statues, chariots, jewelry, stone carvings of birds and animals. She was taken to the most impressive sight she had ever seen. The tomb of Tutankhamen, just recently discovered.

Four gilded shrines, one inside another. Inside the smallest was a sarcophagus with three coffins, the innermost made of

222 pounds of gold. The final resting place of Tutankhamen, an Egyptian pharaoh thirty-three hundred years ago.

In the days that followed, she saw mummy masks and statues of rulers and their retinue, the soldiers and scribes, the working people and writings from each period of history. Writings on parchment, on clay, on stone.

Her favorite statue was of Ramesses II as a child. "He became the ruler of Egypt for over thirty years," said Professor Dasam. "During those years, the height of Egyptian power, he built many monuments including the famous sandstone temples at Abu Simbel. Many believe he was the pharaoh during the exodus of the Jewish people from Egypt," he went on.

Ramesses II didn't look like a child. Behind him stood an enormous falcon. "That is the god, Hurun," said Professor Dasam. "He was a Canaanite god depicted here in the form of a falcon. The disc above the child is Ra, the sun. Mes stands for child as it is written here, stands for the plants he is holding in his hand." Emily had heard of Canaan in her Bible, but she never thought of early gods being shown as animals or birds. Hurun looked very protective of Ramesses.

"Falconry is a very ancient tradition in Arabia," Professor Dasam noted. "These birds are raptors, a type of hawk that is trained to obey his handler and fly at his command. Only the female falcon is used. She will soar above other smaller birds and animals to kill them for the food she needs for her family or for the handler's family. It may seem cruel to you, Emily, but the falcon strikes so quickly there is no pain and the food is always put to good use."

It was time to return to the Lost City. Kadar and Hadar reported to the Professors that the thieves had been freed from jail before they could intercept them. "They may try and return to the Lost City," Hadar advised. "Then your job is to watch over Emily at all costs," said Dasam. "You shall be my Hurun," Emily added to the surprise of Hadar and Kadar and delight of Professor Dasam.

CHAPTER TWELVE:

We Have a Plan

It HAD BEEN several weeks since the thieves had lodged at the Old Oasis Inn at the outskirts of Cairo. The Innkeeper was demanding payment for the rooms. Smiley Wiley told his buddies, "we've got to get some money right away." "How, boss?" asked Nutts. ""We'll sell our jalopy and steal that big roadster the professor came in." "But the driver is always there polishing the brass hub cap and lights," added Rutts. "We'll distract him," said Smiley.

Smiley put on his best English cricket clothes; white trousers, white sneakers and a white shirt with the cuffs rolled up above the elbows just as he had seen the upper class public school boys wear them for this English sport. He approached the driver. ""I say old chap, could you spare a few minutes to help me?" he asked in his best attempt at an upper class diction, "I seem to have misplaced my engine crank." The driver was very obliging. He took the crank from the roadster and followed Smiley beyond a building nearby. As he turned the corner of the building, Butts struck him a blow on the head with a large stone and he fell down unconscious. The thieves took the crank and his cap and sped back to the roadster and drove off to pay the Innkeeper.

"Why pay the innkeeper?" asked Butts.

"You may need a hiding place again, so never cheat another cheat," answered Smiley. When they had paid their bill at the Inn, the four thieves took off for the Lost City in their new roadster. "What a breeze," said Rutts. "Oh for the life of an English gent," said Butts. "Can I sit up front with you?" asked Nutts to Smiley who was driving. "No, Nutthead, can't you see I'm wearing the drivers cap so's people will think you're swells," answered Smiley.

When the luggage for the professors, Emily and her guards was brought where the roadster had been parked, there was nothing there. Where was the roadster and where was the driver. They heard a low moan nearby and upon inspection they found the driver lying next to a nearby building. He slowly sat up and then lay down again. "Look," said Emily, "there's a big lump the size of an orange on the side of his head."

"Easy, easy," said Professor Witherspoon as they helped the driver to his feet. Hadar and Kadar carried him back to Professor Dasam's house, where Apera made him tea. When he recovered he told them about the cricket player needing some help. "I'll bet it was a thief in disguise," said Emily. "If it was, I think we'll find them driving to the Lost City, said Witherspoon. "Then we'll catch them in my Rolls Royce, let's go," said Dasam. They put their luggage in the trunk, together with three extra Gerry cans of petrol as they called gasoline. Professor Dasam drove off, letting the driver recover in a back seat.

Halfway to the Lost City, the stolen roadster began sputtering and then stopped right in the middle of the road. "It's empty, you fools," said Smiley, "we should have checked the fuel gauge." They climbed out of the roadster and pushed it to the side of the road.

Half an hour later a truck was seen approaching. "Nutts," said Smiley, "flag him down." Nutts stood in the middle of the road waving a soiled handkerchief. The truck seemed not to notice as it barreled down the road straight at Nutts, who stood his ground as he had been told. At the last second the truck lurched to the left side of the road and screeched to a stop. An angry Arab got down, screaming at Nutts. Smiley and Rutts and Butts tackled the Arab and tied him up to the roadster with cords from his own clothes. Then they got in the truck and drove off.

Hours later the professors, Emily, her guards and the driver came upon the roadster sitting at the side of the road. An Arab was squatting, tied up next to its front bumper. Dasam spoke to him and got a hasty description of the four thieves and the Arab's truck. They untied him and put him in the Rolls Royce. The driver filled the roadster with gasoline from two of the Gerry cans and he and Witherspoon got in and followed the Rolls Royce towards the Lost City.

It was late at night when they arrived. The full moon shone on the gate posts and nearby they spotted an empty truck. "Allah, Allah," cried the Arab who ran to his truck and began inspecting it inside and outside. He was agitated when he spoke to Professor

Dasam. "The poor man has had all his belongings, his money and his tools stolen," explained Dasam. "I shall reimburse him since it is really our concern that has caused all of this." He gave the man a large sum of money which seemed to please the Arab who embraced Dasam and bowed several times before returning to his truck.

The Rolls Royce and roadster drove through the gates into the Lost City. Several workers were dispatched to keep a close eye on the two cars. Tents were set up but the travelers were too tired to eat. They all washed and went to bed for a well deserved sleep.

A bright sun awoke Emily early. She dressed quickly and went to inspect how much work had been done to unearth the palace. "Emily," a stern voice called out, "have you already forgotten something?" She turned to see Professor Witherspoon outside of his tent still in his pajamas. "Where are Hadar and Kadar, your guards?" he asked. With that Emily spied the two men hastily arranging their garments while they were running towards her. "I'm very sorry, please excuse me," Emily blurted out. "From, now on, if you wish to stay here, you must be sure Hadar and Kadar are nearby," admonished the professor.

That day Emily turned around every few minutes to be sure the guards were nearby. It took away some of the excitement she felt. Kadar approached her with a very large smile. "Little one," he said, "you needn't look for us all the time. Just when you get up. Once you have seen us, we'll stay close by without spoiling your day seeking us." "Thank you, Kadar," she answered.

Two thirds of the palace was now unearthed. It was not unlike others she had seen pictures of in the Museum in Cairo.

The upper stories had friezes, stone pictures, of men and women in various activities, sewing, riding chariots, writing on tablets, standing guard, surrounding the palace's walls. She turned to see the professors approaching. "I can't wait to go inside the palace," she said to them. "Nor can we," they answered. "However, we have something else on our minds."

"We have talked to Hadar and Kadar, and we all agree we are not just going to wait and react to whatever evil plans those thieves cook up. We are going to act, to catch them before they try something sinister. And we have a plan."

CHAPTER THIRTEEN:

Five Years in the Boiler Room

"EMILY HAD A glimpse of the thieves," said Professor Witherspoon, "but the Arab saw them clearly. He even could point out the boss. Let us enlist his aid to describe the thieves." Professor Dasam and the guards approached the Arab who was working on the engine of his truck. They explained their plan and he seemed more than willing to help them. The whole group met in the shade outside Professor Witherspoon's tent. With Dasam translating, each thief was described, including Smiley Wiley the leader, who had a fat round face. "We should be able to identify him," said Emily, "and the one who is totally bald. He is the man who tied me up."

"Now Emily, you are not part of our plan, so please leave us to get on with it," Witherspoon stated. All the men continued to discuss the plan while Emily only overheard glimpses: "night", "disguise", "suborn," "a perfect sting." What did it all mean?

After dinner she went immediately to her tent and, through a small opening, watched as Hadar, Kadar and the Arab retired to Professor Witherspoon's tent. Were they plotting the plan? "It may be tonight," she thought. She put a kerchief over her face and a light cotton coat with a hood covering her body and crept outside barefooted. Soon the men were seen leaving the professor's tent. All were dressed as Arabs and Emily could not even make out which was Professor Witherspoon. They ambled towards the worker's tents. Passing tent after tent, suddenly the lead man stopped and they all stepped back a few paces. Two of the men entered the tent.

Emily's curiosity was too much. She snuck around the back of the tent and listened to the voices of the men inside. "Who are you?" someone spoke out.

"Never mind we are who," a voice answered. "We know you no Arab people. You English people." "What!", another voice answered. "Quiet, please, and listen to what we offer. We a plan have. But we need more people. Like you." "Why us?" asked another voice. "No good you up to. We watch you. Always you follow the rich people who come in Rolls Royce and big roadster. Why do you do that, we ask? Aha, we say. Maybe you steal money or something. We, too, want something. "What do you want?" the first voice inquired. "The parchment paper with the map."

Smiley Wiley had heard enough and he stood up. "I don't know who you Arabs are but we're not interested in stealing a piece of paper with a map of a place we are already standing on." "Do you Arab hieroglyphics read?" a voice responded. Smiley and his henchmen shook their heads. "Much much more is on parchment than just map. On top of palace is secret door to pharaoh's treasure. So secret only parchment can show."

The thieves were hooked. "This must be what they mean by a sting," though Emily. She skirted away from the tent as one of the men leaned against her. "What's that," he said. "What's what?" another asked. "I thought I felt something." "You felt your imagination." They plotted to sneak into Professor Dasam's tent and steal the parchment. The disguised 'Arabs' would keep a lookout from outside while the four thieves went inside and ransacked the tent until they found the paper.

Meanwhile Emily returned to her tent and watched the action from afar. Professor Dasam, Hadar and Kadar and several other men had formed a circle near his tent, all sitting on the ground mumbling words in Arabic. Smiley Wiley looked their way, but saw they were only workers, apparently telling each other stories. The thieves entered the tent and seemed to take hours before they emerged triumphantly with a parchment. "This is not map parchment. Look some more", they were told. When they went inside a second time they found themselves surrounded by Professor Dasam, Hadar, Kadar, the Arab truck driver and several others. "The jig is up," announced Professor Dasam as he uncovered his face. "Secure their hands and feet with good square knots and put them in the back of the truck."

Emily watched it all from a distance and then went inside her tent. That night she slept soundly. In the morning she bounded out of bed and went outside to visit the palace. "Emily," a voice called out. "Have you forgotten to await your guards again?" he went on. "But professor, now that the thieves have …," and she stopped. "Have what?" Professor Witherspoon went on. "Have, have to worry about your plan," she stammered, "I just thought……"

"In fact, my dear, the plan has been executed and the thieves are now tied-up and in our custody. Nevertheless, you await your guards." That was a close call, thought Emily.

With the thieves caught, the professors decided to return to Cairo, place some artifacts they had uncovered with the Museum and get ready for Professor Witherspoon and Emily to return home. Emily walked around dejected. The sparkle in her eyes were dulled with regret. She loved her new dresses and she wanted to spend weeks at the museum. Professor Witherspoon, on the other hand, seemed much more anxious to return home.

"Witherspoon," said Professor Dasam, "your mind seems to be elsewhere. Did something unusual happen on your trip to Egypt? "Unusual, unusual," Witherspoon replied, "why nothing in particular, why do you ask?" "Well, your beaming face reminds me of a naughty boy found with his hand in the cookie jar," Dasam went on. Emily perked up. "Will we be seeing Bibi?" she asked.

"Bibi, who is Bibi. Oh yes, that very attractive tutor you hired to teach Emily French. Do you plan to hire her for the return voyage?" Dasam inquired.

"As a matter of fact, Madam Boissiere has been engaged to tutor Emily on our return," Witherspoon answered with his face reddening. Professor Dasam's eyes lit up. "You old goat. Here you are ten years my senior and in the throes of romance." Emily looked puzzled, was the professor in love?

Preparations for the departure were completed in another week. Professor Dasam's wife had spent most of every day with Emily, at the Museum, at an elegant hairdressers where three women washed and cut her hair and even trimmed her fingernails and toe nails, at the dressmakers where Emily was outfitted with winter clothes, new shoes and a Panama straw hat with a bright yellow ribbon on top. She felt spoiled. How could she thank the Dasam family enough. Maple syrup seemed rather meager in comparison with all the beautiful things Madam Dasam had given her. She looked sad and forlorn.

"My little kitten," Madam Dasam said, looking at Emily's composure. "Why the sad look. Have I spoiled you? I hope so. You are my first daughter and now you are leaving me. I cannot dress you any more. I cannot tell women's secrets to you. Now I must return to rooms full of men and listen to their incessant chatter about business and sports and politics. I shall miss you and I hope that you shall also miss me." Emily flew into the Madam's arms and hugged her and cried. "Of course, I shall miss you, Madam Dasam," she said.

The Rolls Royce, cleaned and polished was driven to the front of Dasam's house where farewells were given and Professor Witherspoon and Emily were driven off. This time they drove to Alexandria, a port city of Egypt where a boat awaited to take them to France. "Can I see the remains of the great library when we get there?" asked Emily. "I'm afraid not," said the Professor. "Alexandria today is a very different city, full of people from all over the Mediterranean, who wish to live in the sun cheaply. For every book now lost there is a bar."

The boat from Alexandria was a cargo ship which carried four staterooms for passengers. Madam Bibi was to meet them in Paris.

Professor Witherspoon and Emily arrived in Paris in early August. They were greeted at the hotel by Madam Bibi, exclaiming, "Ah, mes cheres, relax, for you are with maybe the only French man or woman in Paris. All the rest are tourists."

Tourists?" cried Emily.

"Oui," said Madam Bibi, "It is August and all Frenchmen go on vacation in August. We have free reign of all the museums and Cathedrals, but you will be hearing English and German and Italian and other languages, rarely French and certainly not Parisian French. If only you had arrived last month on the Quatorze!" "Fourteen?" asked Emily.

"Not fourteen, but July Fourteen, the celebration of the successful French Revolution, the beginning of the Republic rather than the Monarchy. Let's pretend and celebrate it is the Fourteenth, no?, professor," she added. "Indeed, we shall," he said.

Back in Cairo, the thieves were tried and convicted of attempted robbery of ancient artifacts. The sentence carried orders to receive five years in prison. Professor Dasam knew that the prisons of Cairo were notorious for unhealthy cells and food. Too many miscreants, people who had broken the law in many different ways, were sick the entire time they were in prison. He arranged that the four thieves would receive in place of a prison cell, daily work in the bowels of an ocean liner shoveling coal into its boilers for the same period of time.

As Emily and Professor Witherspoon were dining on the top deck of the cargo ship, the four thieves were tied up below, to be sent to France and placed aboard the next French Liner leaving from Le Havre.

CHAPTER FOURTEEN:

The True Facts

EMILY, THE PROFESSOR, and Bibi found a small intimate bistro where an accordion player was singing French songs. After they were seated, Bibi excused herself and left the table. Emily spied her talking to the owner of the bistro who smiled and watched as Bibi returned to their table. Suddenly a very solemn march was played by the accordionist and everybody around Emily, including Bibi and the professor, stood up, standing at attention. Emily stood. When the music ended they all clapped and sat down.

"What was that?" asked Emily. "It is the Marseillaise, our national anthem and I shall teach you its words in English and French. You must admit that it is far grander than Mr. Francis Scott Key's?"

"I think the Star Spangled Banner is just as thrilling," protested Emily, although she secretly agreed with Madam Bibi,

Before they left for Le Havre the next morning Madam Bibi strolled along the banks of the Seine with Emily. "Count the bookstalls, mon chere," she said. "You can determine how civilized a city is by its number of book stores." "You must come to our house, then," Emily replied, "it is all books." Madam Bibi gave her a curious look. Was Emily teasing her?

They took a first class compartment in the train from Paris to Le Havre. It had its own special door inside and outside the train, plush velvet seats but not room for the luggage, which was in a special luggage car attached to the train. Emily watched the countryside roll by. Every piece of earth was under some cultivation. Fields of red poppies, yellow sunflowers, vegetables, walnut trees, vineyards swept by. "France has been called the breadbasket of Europe," Professor Witherspoon noted. "A small country by our size, it uses every inch of soil to grow something."

That night they stayed at a small inn run by an elderly couple who offered a glass of wine to Emily along with the professor and Madam Bibi. The professor looked taken back until Madam Bibi said in French, "the young lady would like it watered down, if you please." When it was returned the dark red color looked a dull pink, but Emily felt very grown up with her glass of wine. "This will be our little secret, no?" said Madam Bibi. "Oui," answered Emily in her best French.

Next morning they found themselves in the very same state rooms they had on sailing to Europe. Emily's porter explained that the French Line prided itself on keeping records of every passenger that sailed with them. "Maybe you would like to see the whole ship?" he inquired. "We have an Engineer's tour on Tuesdays." Emily told him she would ask Madam Bibi, but was sure the answer would be yes.

Tuesday morning, all three took the tour. There were seven stages, floors, with passenger rooms. The top two were First Class, the next two Cabin Class. She was on the upper of the two cabin class floors. Below that were three Tourist Class floors. Aft, or behind the tourist rooms, were the galleys where cooks prepared more than a thousand meals for every sitting. A sitting was the time when one was obliged to eat. Emily already knew that hers would be the last, the "civilized" last as Madam Bibi would say. Outside Emily's floor was a promenade deck. Four times around was about one mile. Food was stored more forward on the ship. Some 60,000 eggs would be used during the voyage.

Steam turbines powered the ocean liner and at the very bottom of the boat was the boiler room where Emily watched men bare to the waist, with handkerchiefs wound around their foreheads, shovel coal into furnaces belching hot air from the fires inside. "Look," professor, "that man, third from the right, isn't that Smiley Wiley?" "And the bald man next to him?" "What on earth," said the professor. "I shall certainly inquire about the names of the men working here."

That night they were invited to sit at the Purser's table. "This is an honor, Emily," said Professor Witherspoon. The Captain entertains a select few of the First Class passengers just as the Purser selects a few of the Cabin Class passengers. So best bib and tucker." Emily chose her favorite dress that Madam Dasam had made for her. Madam Bibi, too, was dressed to the nines, as the professor said, and he was in black tie and tuxedo. "Mon chere, let me fix your tie, it is so crooked," said Bibi as she reached up on the tips of her toes, straightening his bow tie and giving him a short peck on his cheek.

The professor told the Purser about the thieves they uncovered in Egypt. They looked like several of the men in the boiler room. The Purser noted that it was surely a mistake, a coincidental appearance, but that he would check out the names. At breakfast the professor and Emily ate alone, as Madam Bibi thought it barbaric to eat all that food so early in the day. The Purser showed the professor and Emily a list of names of the men working in the boiler room. There they were: Smiley Wiley, Butts Noggin, Rutts Noggin and Nutts Noggin. "Oh dear, oh dear," said Witherspoon. "These are the men I spoke of. I know they were brought before the court in Cairo."

"I shall check with the Captain for an explanation," said the purser. He returned quite quickly. "This will seem unusual to you. I know it is very strange to me, I have never heard of such a thing before. A Professor Dasam requested that the Court in Cairo change the sentence from five years in prison to five years in the boiler room of an ocean liner under strict supervision. The court obliged and the French line agreed. The Captain asked if you would join him at lunch on the Main Deck to explain further." "We would be delighted," said the professor.

Although it was the first sitting, Madam Bibi was too curious to see how the First Class passengers lived not to join them at the Captain's table. In this circumstance it was a very small table for six. The Captain, his First Mate, the Purser and the three of them. "I am really at a loss for words, Professor," said the Captain. It seems that this Professor Dasam is a personal friend of the owners of the French Line, in fact I believe Dasam has shares in the corporation." "Shares?" asked Emily. "The French Line is a corporation, a company. Individuals and other companies own part of the corporation with what we call shares."

"Anyway, Dasam's request was accepted." "Well," said Professor Witherspoon, "the professor is also a very close personal friend of mine. In fact he was with us at the capture of those men. There must be a good reason for his request. I just hope and pray that you guard them carefully. They are very clever men."

In fact, as the Captain was talking, those clever men were plotting how to get out of the infernal boiler room. Each had lost at least five pounds in just the first few days on board, shoveling coal into the fiery boilers. "We've got one thing going for us," said Smiley. "What's that? asked Butts. "We're all working the same shift. That's the one time we are all watched. I think we've got to figure out an escape at nighttime." They slept on hammocks over the screws, the huge propellers on steel poles the width of a tree trunk, that drove the ocean liner. Just fore of them was the laundry. "When the room is full of snoring boiler workers and the noise of the screws is at full blast, we'll sneak into the laundry and exchange our clothes for those of stewards."

That night around three am, the four thieves tip-toed out of their bunk room into the laundry. Dozens and dozens of machines were washing and drying clothes. They stopped two in a wash cycle and used sheets to clean themselves from dirt and grime of coal dust. They put their dirty clothes into the machine and turned it back on. Naked they snuck around the room looking for newly pressed stewards' clothes. Several times they hid as a laundress came by with soiled linens. There, ahead of them were women ironing sheets, pillows, linen and shirts. Nearby were trousers and coats, hanging on steel poles.

Smiley saw a brush laying by his feet. He picked it up and three it across the room. "A rat!" he exclaimed loudly. The women screamed and ran from the room. Quickly the men grabbed shirts and ties and socks and coats and suits and underwear and left the room. Between the four they were able to assemble steward's clothes with a reasonable fit if one didn't look too closely. They found a stairwell that ran up all the floors to the First Class main deck. When they got there the door was locked. They went down to Cabin Class. That door, too, was locked. So they sat down on the steps not knowing what to do.

A steward came scampering up the stairwell. "You late, too?" he asked in French. Smiley nodded, since he didn't know what the steward said. The steward took out a key. It looked more like a bolt. It was long and the end was filed into four sides which slid into the door lock. Turning the key opened the door and the five men ran up to First Class where the key also opened the door. Smiley 'accidentally' bumped the steward when he opened the door and Rutts pick pocketed the steward's key into his own trousers. The men knocked on doors until they found a room with no reply. A maid approached and in French explained that the cabin was empty. When Smiley looked confused she took out another key and opened the cabin door pointing to the empty room. Smiley tried the bump again but the maid slapped him in the face and while Smiley opened his arms in sincere regrets,

Rutts slipped his hand into the maid's gown and extracted a set of keys. She stomped off in a fit.

"We had better look for an empty cabin elsewhere, away from that 'battle axe'," suggested Butts. The thieves went down the stairs to Cabin Class, where they found another empty cabin. The set of keys apparently opened all of the doors. "We'll settle in here," said Smiley. "But how will we eat?" asked Nutts. "Lots of passengers eat in their state rooms. They put what they don't finish outside their door. We'll eat that," said Smiley.

It wasn't long into the day before the men were missing from their work shift. Filthy clothes had left stains on linen in the laundry room and several stewards were asking for their coats and trousers. When this was reported to the Captain he was enraged. "Somewhere among thousands of passengers and crew are four henchmen, probably dressed as stewards, but who knows what steps they are taking right now before our eyes to deceive us further?" he commanded.

"I do not want our passengers to hear about this. It will unduly frighten them. These men are not killers, they are thieves. So we must suggest that passengers be especially wary of leaving valuables where they might be purloined. In any voyage there may be, among the passengers, men or women who use the relaxed nature of an ocean voyage to steal. Just as we warn the passengers about card sharks, people who will cheat at playing bridge or poker."

Taking the purser aside he added, "but we must tell the true facts to the professor and his party.

CHAPTER FIFTEEN:

A Trick Overdone

THE NEWS OF the escaped thieves was received with some trepidation. Professor Witherspoon asked the Captain how they could insure Emily's safety, since the thieves had tried to kidnap her in Egypt. "This is a difficult problem," said the Captain. "We are happy to provide you with two stewards who will keep a close eye on her, but the stewards will not be armed." Emily spoke up, "Professor, we know the thieves are on the ship, but they do not know we are here, also." "We shall take no chances anyway," the Captain went on.

"It appears that the thieves are hidden somewhere in Cabin Class," the Captain said, " so if it is all right with you, I shall move all three of you to First Class, where it will be easier to keep a watch for anything that might appear unusual." This was readily agreed to, especially by Madam Bibi who discovered that the last sitting in First Class was even later than in Cabin Class.

Steamer trunks and other personal items were moved without

incident and two young and very handsome stewards were assigned to keep watch over Emily. They showed her the First Class swimming pool which included the largest towel Emily had ever seen. It wrapped around her twice from head to toe; she looked more like a mummy than a young girl. On the promenade deck there was skeet shooting. Black plate-like discs were tossed out into the ocean and men and women tried to hit them with shot guns. When they hit a plate it would shatter into a hundred pieces dropping into the ocean. Further on were shuffle board matches. On the floor were squares and rectangles marked with numbers 5, 10, 30, 50. Contestants held long poles that spread out at the end with a curved flat wooden edge abutting round shuffles or discs. By pushing the disc forward towards the squares and rectangles, people tried to land a disc on a square with a high number. Most landed outside or beyond any of the squares.

Back in Cabin Class, Smiley and his gang were restless. The two beds in their cabin were too small for more than one person, so they took turns sleeping. The fact that there was no soap or toothpaste didn't bother them. They rarely washed their bodies or their teeth anyway. But they were bored just sitting around, hidden in the empty cabin. One or another was forever leaving the state room in search of a food tray outside another room's door. By now they had accumulated fifteen trays and were tired of eating leftovers, cold coffee, luke warm tea, stale breads with marmalades and strawberry preserves.

"I'm going up to First Class," said Butts. "There's gotta be something better to eat up there." "Well, keep your eyes peeled and come back soon," replied Smiley. Butts took the steward's pass key and went up the stairs to First Class. The top floor was empty of discarded food trays, but on the lower one he spied a large platter with smoked salmon, peeled shrimp and even a half full bottle of red wine. As he was picking up the tray he bumped into a small lady. "Excuse me," he said in English.

"Do I look English to you," the lady responded in a French accent. He bowed his head and left her standing, staring at him. He didn't mention the incident as the four men devoured the leftovers from the large platter. "Well done, Butts," said Smiley as he grabbed the wine bottle from Nutts' hands, "a feast fit for four gentlemen travelers."

Professor Witherspoon, Madam Bibi and Emily were sunning themselves in lounge chairs, reading books and magazines. "Ernest," said Madam Bibi, "I saw the strangest steward this morning. He was well dressed but had on the dirtiest shoes one could imagine. They looked more like workman's brogans than the highly polished shoes of a steward. And he was not very observant. He inadvertently bumped me and apologized in English. English, can you imagine. If you will excuse me, dear Emily, I really do not like being compared to an English lady in her dowdy hats and dresses."

"He must have been one of the thieves," said Emily. "They couldn't change their shoes even though they dressed as stewards." "What was he doing?" she asked Madam Bibi. "He was collecting an empty tray from outside the door of a stateroom," she replied. "Well, I doubt he was a thief, then," Professor Witherspoon added. Emily thought more about it. Why the dirty shoes. Why speak English to Madam Bibi who was so French in dress and manner.

"The tray, was it completely empty?" Emily went on. "Oh I

Gerry Hotchkiss

do not know. I just presumed it was empty since it was outside the door waiting to be removed." "Suppose it had food on it," said Emily. "If the thieves are hiding, where will they get food except from leftovers?"

"Now that's clear thinking," Professor Witherspoon commented. "We shall talk to the Captain about this."

The Captain's First Mate, listened intently to Emily's surmise. "Let us set a trap," he suggested. 'We shall leave a large platter with lots of leftovers and two partially full bottles of red wine. But I will drill a small hole in the bottom and leave enough spilled wine on the platter that it will drip as the tray is carried away." "What a first class idea," said the professor. "Maybe that's why he is the First Mate," joked Emily. They all laughed and plotted the trap for that very night.

Smiley Wiley was so happy with Butts' provisions, he decided he would do the honors that evening. He put his steward's coat on, buttoning it tightly against his protruding belly and smoothed his hair with small gobs of grease from the door hinges to the bathroom. Taking the pass key he went up to First Class. Not far away he spied the tray filled with so many left overs. What a catch! He picked up the tray and sped back to the thieves' state room below.

There were leftovers of roast duck, green beans, potatoes, steak, artichokes, asparagus, several cheeses, butter, fresh rolls and crackers. There was even a half filled small bowl of caviar. When they had had their fill, their bellies full, the four men lay around on the two beds celebrating their extraordinary good luck. "What was those little black things I ate," asked Nutts, "kinda fishy tasting, but good."

"That was caviar, Beluga caviar, the most expensive thing you can eat," answered Smiley. But then he sat straight up. "It's a trap!" he cried. 'Nobody would leave uneaten caviar on a tray." He opened the door to the hallway. He looked up and down. Nobody was there. As he closed the door he saw the spots of red wine on the floor. He followed them, leading him right to the stairs to the First Class state rooms.

He rushed back. "Collect your things. We've been discovered. I doubt they'll do anything until the morning. We'll hide out in one of the lifeboats under the tarpaulins," he told the others. "What boats?" asked Nutts.

"Didn't you see them. On both sides of the liner. They're there in case we had to abandon the ship, like when it hits an ice berg and the passengers are taken to safety in the smaller boats," Smiley explained. The tarpaulins of the first two boats they climbed up to were so tightly roped they could not climb inside the boat. But the third was loose and the four men easily hid inside.

Following the spots of wine, in the early morning the First Mate and several stewards went right to the cabin the thieves had used. Opening the door, they found it empty but for piles of trays without a scrap of food on them. There was the platter with the small hole in it. On it lay empty dishes, empty wine bottles and even the elegant empty caviar dish. The First Mate stared at the dish. He had ordered a steward to fill the platter with partially eaten food fit for a rich passenger. Had he included a dish of caviar? "I think I know what has happened," he announced, "our trick was a bit overdone."

CHAPTER SIXTEEN:

A Very Long Story

"WE ARE CHECKING every unused state room twice a day and once a night," said the Captain, "and all stewards will wear an employee name tag on the front of their coats for the two days left of this voyage." He hoped that this would limit any activities of the thieves, wherever they might be hiding. Had he known how worried the four men actually were, his extra precautions could have been dismissed.

As it was, the four remained under the tarpaulin without food or water as silent as the smooth and silken sea half an hour before sunset.

To cheer Emily up, her stewards asked her if she had ever seen the green flash. "Green flash," she asked, "what is that?" "As the sun sets to the West on a calm sea such as this one, just as the sun goes down beyond the horizon you can see a green flash - just for a split second," they explained. To get the very best look, the stewards got permission for Emily to visit the Captain's control room on the top deck.

Several men were busy at wheels and levers and behind them was a square table with rulers and pins placed on several maps. The Captain was studying one such map as Emily entered. "Here to see the green flash, I believe," he said. Emily smiled as he lifted her up onto a high chair that overlooked an expanse of ocean to the West. She felt silly. She could easily have climbed into that seat herself. Watch carefully now," he went on, "the flash will be here any second." "There it is!"

Emily saw no green flash. Did she miss it or were these officers just kidding her. "Did you see it?" they asked. "See it, why if we were heading East, it would have covered Ireland," she answered, thinking "this must be what Professor Witherspoon calls a 'white lie'." In any case, the answer seemed to satisfy the crew.

The morning the Ile de France arrived in New York, a tug boat greeted them at the end of the 'narrows', a stretch of the Hudson River that flows into the Atlantic Ocean. It was called a pilot boat, because the captain of the ferry boat was responsible to pilot the massive ocean liner up the narrows into the piers on the West side of the Island of Manhattan.

"He and the Captain work together to insure that the liner follows a true path to its docking. It is a very precise operation. For example when the Captain turns the liner in any direction, including stopping, he gives his orders minutes before the ship actually turns or stops," the purser explained to Emily.

When the great ship stopped, small lines were thrown ashore to be caught by deckhands on the pier. They took the lines which held huge ropes the thickness of an arm and tied the ropes around giant winches, circular iron poles with cranks to turn the ropes around them. Finally the ship was secured to the pier and gangways, ladders fifty feet or more in length, were rolled down from the deck to the pier.

As Emily disembarked with Madam Bibi and the professor, the Captain gave her a small package, saying "merci", thanks, for her ingenuity in attempting to catch the thieves. Awaiting the steamer trunks, Emily opened the package. In it was a dark blue sailor's cap with a red and white ribbon of the French Line. She placed it on her head. A perfect fit.

"We have another surprise for you," said the professor. "I hope you don't mind that we did this without your permission or attendance. Last night the Captain, with the legal rights he has to do such things, married Madam Bibi and I. May I be the first to introduce you to Mrs. Wither spoon." "And from now on, mon chere, you shall just call me Aunt Bibi!" Mrs. Witherspoon added.

"But I have no present to give you," blurted Emily. "Newly married couples always are given presents." "My dearest," said the professor, "you are a present enough for twenty couples. But if you must give us one, I have a suggestion. That you always call us Uncle Ernest and Aunt Bibi. Although we really are not your blood relatives, we feel we are even closer than that." Emily ran over and hugged both new relatives with tears of joy streaming down all their faces.

Awaiting them past the customs office, where their passports were checked and stamped, were Emily's mother and father. Her mother held her so tight and so long and longer still, Emily felt she might faint. "Sarah," said her father, "let go and give someone else a chance to say hello." "Hush," said her mother, "I may never let go." But she did as Emily's father picked her up, held her at arms length and stared at her in what looked like a most serious study. "Sarah, I'm not sure this is our Emily, what do you think?" And then he winked and hugged her harder if not longer than her mother had.

In the stern, the rear, of the liner, Smiley Wiley and his henchmen crawled out of the boat in which they were hiding and crept towards the side against the pier. They spotted one of the thick ropes that secured the ship to the shore and, hand over hand, they slid down the rope and onto the pier. Then they quietly held on to the pier and jumped into the water. They swam away from the pier with the building housing the customs office and found another docking place unattended. Wet and cold, they crawled up a rope ladder onto its walkway and slipped away.

"Daddy," Emily said in the most stern voice she could muster without giggling, "Professor Witherspoon has been..." and then with a French accent she went on, "a naughty boy. He has married Madam Bibi."

"Congratulations to both of you," said her father. "No, no, William, we congratulate the husband and offer good wishes to his wife," her mother corrected. "Why," asked Emily. "Because you congratulate the man on his good fortune in getting this lovely lady to be his wife and you offer good wishes to the lady that her choice will be as fortunate," her mother answered. Emily's puzzled look was interrupted by the new Mrs. Witherspoon, "Mon chere, the fortune is both ours together with our brand new relative, our only niece, Emily."

Over dinner at her father's university club, Ernest and Bibi and Emily began to tell her parents what would become a very long story.

Further adventures of Emily to be published.

Emily
in
Khara-Koto

CHAPTER ONE:

A Chinese dinner it will be

THE MONTHS OF school rushed by. Emily found her favorite subjects were geography and English. Geography because it talked of far away lands and English because the better she read the more books she could enjoy about places like Machu Picchu in Peru and Ulan Bator in Mongolia.

"I'm afraid she'll never be satisfied with the simple life of New England," said her mother, Sarah. "All she talks about are the mountains of Peru or the deserts of Mongolia."

"You don't think Mount Desert, Maine will suffice?" responded her father.

"Well, it's really all your fault, you and your father and Professor Witherspoon," her mother went on. "That adventure in Arabia makes a map in school look like an artifact from the bronze age."

It was true. The blackboard and the maps that hung from several walls, the desks and ink wells with a small slot to put away books and papers were hardly the stuff of uncovering an ancient city like Urgup. Her teacher, Miss Osgood, was always enthusiastic. She gave her heart and soul to her classroom. Emily memorized poems and psalms from the Bible. She recited the names of the capital of the forty-eight states, even Helena, Montana and Albany, New York. But she dreamed of more exotic places where people lived very different lives. On her report card, to her marks Miss Osgood added: "at times it appears as if Emily is somewhere else, far, far away."

As April passed and the summer months were approaching, Emily's mother looked over brochures for summer camps. Lakes and mountains, fresh air, swimming, canoeing, hiking, sailing, arts and crafts were spelled out in glowing terms. "William, if we are serious about Emily going to camp for eight weeks this summer, we need to get on the ball right now." Her father, who was usually overly organized, seemed to be dawdling about Emily's summer plans. "We've got plenty of time, Sarah," he answered.

"Plenty of time. It will be May next week and just ten weeks until these camps open up,"her mother reminded him.

Emily looked at the brochures. All the photos showed happy girls in their smocks or woolen swimsuits, enjoying a camp's facilities. "Under the Pines," "Above the Waterfall," "Ghost Stories at the Campfire." read captions under the pictures. Tame stuff compared to climbing down a well in Egypt, or driving through the sands of a desert in a new Rolls Royce.

"William," said her mother a week later, "no more procrastinating. Let's both of us and Emily choose a camp and be done with it." Her father looked sheepish. "I may have an alternative," he said. "Alternative?" her mother replied. "Well, not exactly a camp alternative. More of an adventure alternative. A trip to China."

If Emily's eyes opened any wider they would have popped out right there on the spot.

"China," her mother said in desperation, why don't you and I discuss this privately, away from our daughter," she added as she stacked the camp brochures in a pile on a table nearby. "Let's take a stroll outside." Emily watched her mother and father walk down the street and followed them at a safe distance. She couldn't hear what they were saying but watched their body movements for answers. At first her mother waved her arms, stopped once and seemed just to glare at her father. Then they ambled on, talking more calmly. When her father put his arm around her mother and her mother leaned more closely to him, Emily smiled. Maybe China will be my summer's vacation, she mused.

She sped back home undetected and pretended to be reading a book as he parents opened the screen door and entered the house. "I am willing to wait for the professor's letter," she heard her mother say, "but only for one week."

One week. Either a camp in New Hampshire or a trip to China. It was too much to bear. Emily went to the library, where he mother was the librarian, to look in the section of books on China. There were so many. History, culture, politics, trade, religion, education, medicine. Where would she start. She looked at a map. China was vast, too big to study all of it. Where did the professor plan to travel in China. She left without any books, more confused than ever. She would have to await the professor's letter.

She asked Miss Osgood about China. "As a matter of fact," said her teacher, "you've come to the right place. My brother is an anthropologist and his special interest happens to be the Far East." "What part of China interests you, Emily," she added. "Something ancient," was all Emily could think of.

"That's not very specific, young lady. China is a very ancient country with a history that goes back more than five thousand years. Did you know that the Chinese invented gun powder? Maybe you should just start with a dinner at Chin Chow's downtown and ask the Chows," she joked.

Emily's parents rarely ate out. How could she get them to the Chows, she pondered.

"Well, pumpkin," her father asked that evening. " what did you learn in school today?"

"We discussed foods from around the world," Emily made up. "Do they sound better than home cooking?" added her mother as she entered the room. "I don't know, I've never tasted foreign food, answered Emily.

"Well, we can change that," said her father. "Why don't we all go to dinner tomorrow night at Chin Chow's downtown, I've heard that children like Chinese food as much as adults," he went on."

"It is time for Seth to improve his table manners," her mother added. Her younger brother was notorious for his sloppy table habits, like not unfolding his napkin or eating his vegetables and spilling his milk.

"That's settled, a Chinese dinner it all be," announced her father.